THE BLACK MASK LIBRARY

THE EARLY YEARS (1920–26)

The Man in the Shadows: The Complete Black Mask
Cases of Terry Mack *by Carroll John Daly*

THE SHAW YEARS (1926–36)

Blood on the Curb *by Joseph T. Shaw*

Black Harvest: The Complete Black Mask
Cases of Jules Tremaine *by Norvell W. Page*

Boomerang Dice: The Complete Black Mask Cases of
Johnny Hi Gear *by Stewart Sterling*

Dead Evidence: The Complete Black Mask Cases of
Harrigan *by Ed Lybeck*

Laughing Death *by Raoul Whitfield*

Luck: The Complete Black Mask Cases of
Oscar Sail *by Lester Dent*

The Price of a Dime: The Complete Black Mask Cases of
Ben Shaley *by Norbert Davis*

South Wind: The Complete Black Mask Cases of
Jerry Tracy *by Theodore Tinsley*

THE LATER YEARS (1936–51)

Dead and Done For: The Complete Black Mask Cases of
Cellini Smith *by Robert Reeves*

Let the Dead Alone: The Complete Black Mask Cases of
Luther McGavock *by Merle Constiner*

Murder Costs Money: The Complete Black Mask Cases
of Rex Sackler *by D.L. Champion*

THE PRICE OF A DIME

The Complete

Cases of Ben Shaley

NORBERT DAVIS

---

introduction by Bob Byrne

illustrations by Arthur Rodman Bowker

cover by Jes Schlaikjer

BLACK MASK

2021

Table of Contents

Introduction

LIKE MANY OF his contemporaries, Norbert Davis wrote for different outlets, including for the Westerns, war stories, and even romance markets. But he was at his best in the private eye/mystery field. Davis could write standard hardboiled fare, but he excelled at mixing humor into the genre. Unfortunately (and aided and abetted by his wonderful Doan and Carstairs novels), that has left the skewed view that he could only write screwball hardboiled stories. And that's simply not accurate.

Davis was a law student at Stanford when "The Bonded Stuff" appeared in the March, 1932 issue of *Real Detective*. A mere three months later in June, his first submission to *Black Mask*, "Reform Racket," saw print. Davis continued writing, and after he graduated in 1934, he never bothered to take the bar exam: A career in the pulps beckoned instead.

Though Joe 'Cap' Shaw, legendary editor of *Black Mask*, accepted that first submission, he didn't feel that Davis' hardboiled humor really fit the magazine. So, even with a home run in his first at-bat, the writer only managed to break into *Black Mask* a total of five times during the years of Shaw's reign: 1932–1937. Davis had success in other markets, however, with eighteen mystery stories seeing print in 1936, for example. And several stories appeared in *Black Mask* after Shaw departed. Davis later 'moved up' to the higher-paying, more respectable, glossy slicks.

In "Reform Racket," Dan Stiles returns to an unnamed town. A local crook named Bradford wants to pay Stiles for protection; his brother-in-law Georgeson offers him an unasked-for blackmail payment; and a cop named Raimler says he's quitting his job and 'throwing in' with Stiles. The rub is that Stiles has absolutely no idea why he's so popular. We don't know why he left town (though he indicates he was unpopular when he departed), why he came back, or why everybody has an agenda concerning him.

But Ramlier reveals that Georgeson is about to be picked as the reform candidate for mayor. And since the would-be-future mayor is married to Stiles' sister, that makes Stiles an important man: Or so people think. He realizes Georgeson thought that he was hitting him up for money to depart— along with his notorious past—so that Stiles wouldn't embarrass him during the election.

Davis tangles together Bradford, Georgeson, and Ramlier in a web of crime, a reform platform, and Stiles being proactive, rather than reactive. Many years before Raymond Chandler famously said "When in doubt, have a man come through a door with a gun in his hand," that's exactly what Davis does in this story. Two men, actually.

This ten-page story is divided into seven numbered parts. Six pages and six parts are the set-up. I think that Shaw bought this one for the last four pages, which is the seventh and final part. It's an action-packed finale, with four guns and five people getting shot. And we get character reveals for everybody of note. Davis poured everything into the climax and denouement. And it's the ending that carries the story. Except for a few wise-cracks from Ramlier, there's no humor in this story. While Davis' enduring reputation is one of writing comedies, he regular wrote 'straight' hardboiled, starting right out of the gate.

"Reform Racket" was the one and only appearance for Dan Stiles. Davis did write some recurring characters, with Bail Bond Dodd leading the pack, appearing eight times. But there was no Cardigan, or Jo Gar, or even a Bill Brent. Most of his characters were one and done. Fortunately, a few did make return engagements. It would be a full year before Davis returned to *Black Mask,* with a semi-detective, in "Kansas City Flash" in the March, 1933 issue.

Another one-off hero, Mark Hull, is our protagonist this time around. Hull is sort of a free-lance Bill Lennox. A former movie stunt-man, he hires out to studios for 'hush-hush' jobs. Hull is tough and, frankly, unlikable. The only reason the reader is rooting for him is because he's looking for a kidnapped actress. As a writer, Davis would excel at depth in his supporting characters. The five Max Latin stories are populated with superb ones. But that came later, after Davis refined his skills. Even the damsel in distress isn't captivating.

Once again, it's the action-packed finale which is the story's strength. And this one doesn't involve guns. We also learn the reason behind the story's title during the final confrontation.

This one has even less humor than "Reform Racket." Hull does make a joke to get rid of a nosy old lady, but he doesn't toss off quips, and nobody else is funny. Hull is a one-dimensional tough guy.

The pattern established, it was about a year before Shaw saw fit to print another Davis story, but it was worth the wait. "Red Goose" graced the February, 1934 issue.

"Shaley was bonily tall. He had a thin, tanned face with bitterly heavy lines in it. He looked calm; but he looked like he was being calm on purpose—as though he was consciously holding himself in. He had an air of hardboiled confidence."

Side note: Pulpsters were paid by the word. And not well. Clearly, Davis saw adverbs as a way to wring a few more pennies out of each story. You really notice it in the terrific Max Latin stories. But once you realize it, you can't help but see adverbs all over the place in his work. There's nothing wrong with that (Mark Twain and Stephen King excepted)—but it's tough to ignore after you become aware of it.

This was a much more competent Norbert Davis than the version which authored "Kansas City Flash." In fact, I think you can point to "Red Goose" as the beginning of his career as a first-rate pulpster.

Once again, the humor that Davis is best known for is mostly absent from this story. But the exasperation Shaley shows with the fussy, humorless museum curator is pretty amusing. Reading "Red Goose" as a 'straight' hardboiled story, this one shows that he was mastering the form. Keep in mind we're only two years removed from his first publication.

Shaley agrees to find a painting from the 1500s, which had been cut out of the frame while the guards were distracted by a staged fight elsewhere in the museum. The museum will pay up to $5,000 for its safe return, which is a lot of money for the time. Davis incorporates the boxing scene, the art world, and a gang of thieves without honor, and packs them into this short tale. It's well-crafted pulp with something of a twist at the end.

One thing I've noticed about Davis: villains get roughed up. In pulp stories, the heroes get worked over and shot—so do the bad guys. And this applies to women. If you believe someone should never strike a woman, you probably shouldn't read Davis:

He picked her up by the front of her dress and slapped her in the face—quick, sharp slaps rocked her head back and forth.

You can read the story and decide if she deserved that. But a villain gets what they have coming, regardless of gender. That's just the state of things in those pulp days. I don't have too much sympathy for the antagonists who are on the receiving end of what they deserve, male or female. It's a rough and dangerous game.

Davis writes an action-packed final confrontation (did you expect anything else?) with Shaley and four others in one room of an apartment. There's punching, strangling, and shooting, all in one chaotic scene. Shaley manages to get out alive and ends up back where he started, in the curator's office, the case solved. Or is it?

A 1952 episode of the television show *Suspense* featured Shaley and the credits state that it was based on a Norbert Davis story. *The Blue Panther* certainly change some things, but it was clearly based on "Red Goose."

"Red Goose" should be read by anyone who simply dismisses Davis as the hardboiled guy that wrote with too much humor (which is an inaccurate viewpoint to begin with). Raymond Chandler said that "Red Goose" impressed him more than any other tale he read when he decided to become a hardboiled writer. That's a fairly authoritative recommendation!

Shaw (grudgingly, one suspects) included "Red Goose" in his legendary *Hard Boiled Omnibus* compilation. In an unpublished introduction to the story, Shaw wrote, "There is one thing that makes Bert Davis an individualist; he always did and always will write just what he very well pleases: mostly what strikes him as 'funny'."

Shaley made his only other appearance just two months later in "The Price of a Dime."

Shaley's secretary, Sadie, would have been an entertaining character if the series had gone on. She is trying to forcibly remove a large blonde woman from the office as this tale opens. It's another scene where Davis shows he could write humor without going overboard. The woman's brother, a bellhop of questionable integrity, is going to be arrested for some hotel shenanigans, and she wants Shaley to help.

A crazy, violent escapade follows, with a Hollywood director in the middle of it all. At one point, when things go a bit poorly, someone says of an angry Shaley, "No, he gets that way when he's mad. And when he's mad, he's a great big dose of bad medicine for somebody." That doesn't bode well for the bad guy.

Unlike "Red Goose," this story ends with a chase scene and a shootout—on the lot of a western movie. And Norbert Davis never again wrote any stories about his Los Angeles detective.

Shaley isn't one of the great hardboiled private eyes, but Davis wrote two good stories about him, and the P.I. represented 40% of his success in making sales to Joe Shaw at *Black Mask*. One wonders why he didn't write a few more Shaley tales, which he could reasonably have expected Shaw to buy. Davis was still a young writer in the field, and appearing in *Black Mask* would certainly help him sell to other magazines. And even though eight of his stories were accepted by the magazine post-Shaw, he never revisited Shaley.

So, enjoy Norbert Davis' earliest work in *Black Mask*. And look for volume two, with the remaining 'Shaw-approved' stories. And let's face it: you can trust Raymond Chandler's recommendation, can't you?

Red Goose

The picture was framed—and so was everyone in the deal

IT WAS A long, high-ceilinged hall, gloomy and silent. The air was musty. Tall, barred windows on one side of the hall let in a little of the bright sunlight where it formed waffle-like patterns on the thick green carpet. There was a polished brass rail, waist-high, running the length of the hall on the side opposite the barred windows.

Shaley came quietly along the hall. He was whistling softly to himself through his teeth and tapping with his forefinger on the brass rail in time with his steps.

Shaley was bonily tall. He had a thin, tanned face with bitterly heavy lines in it. He looked calm; but he looked like he was being calm on purpose—as though he was consciously holding himself in. He had an air of hardboiled confidence.

A door at the end of the hall opened, and a wrinkled little man in a gray suit that was too big for him came hurrying out. He carried a framed picture under one arm, and had dusty, rimless glasses on the end of his nose. He had a worried, absent-minded expression on his face, and mumbled in a monotone to himself.

Shaley stepped in front of him and said: "Hello."

"How do you do," said the little man busily. He didn't look up. He tried to side-step around Shaley.

Shaley kept in front of him. "My name is Shaley—Ben Shaley."

"Yes, yes," said the little man absently. "How do you do, Mr. Shaley." He tried to squeeze past.

Shaley put out one long arm, barring his way.

"Shaley," he said patiently. "Ben Shaley. You sent for me."

The little man looked up, blinking through the dusty glasses. "Oh!" he said. "Oh! Mr. Shaley. Of course. You're the detective."

Shaley nodded. "Now you're getting it."

The little man made nervous, batting gestures with one hand, blinking. Apparently he was trying to remember why he had sent for a detective.

"Oh, yes!" he said, snapping his fingers triumphantly. "The picture! Yes, yes. My name is Gray, Mr. Shaley. I'm the curator in charge. Won't you step into my office?"

"Thanks," said Shaley.

Gray trotted quickly back down the hall, back through the

door. It was a small office with a big, flat desk next to another barred window. Gray dodged around the desk and sat down in the chair behind it, still holding the framed picture.

Shaley sat down in another chair, tipped it back against the wall, and extended his long legs comfortably.

Gray held up the picture and stared at it admiringly, head on one side. "Beautiful, isn't it?" he asked, turning the picture so Shaley could see it.

"Too fat," said Shaley.

Gray blinked. "Fat?" he said, bewilderedly.

"It's a picture of a dame, isn't it?" Shaley asked.

"It's a nude," Gray admitted.

Shaley nodded. "She's too fat. She bulges."

"Bulges?" Gray repeated in amazement. "Bulges?" He looked from the picture to Shaley. "Why, this is a Rubens."

Shaley tapped his fingers on the arm of his chair. "I suppose you had some reason for calling me?"

Gray came out of his daze. "Oh, yes. Yes, yes. It was about the picture."

"What picture? This one?"

"Oh, no. The one that was stolen."

Shaley took a deep breath. "Now we're getting somewhere. There was a picture stolen?"

"Of course," said Gray. "That's why I called you."

"I'm glad to know that. When was it stolen?"

"Three days ago. Mr. Denton recommended you. Mr. Denton is one of the trustees of the museum."

"Denton, the lawyer?"

Gray nodded. "Mr. Denton is an attorney. He said something about setting a crook to catch a crook."

"I'll remember that," said Shaley.

"I hope I haven't offended you?" Gray said anxiously.

"You better hope so," Shaley told him. "I'm bad medicine when I get offended. There was a picture stolen from the museum, then, three days ago. What kind of picture?"

"The *Red Goose,* painted by Guiterrez about 1523. A beautiful thing. It was loaned to us by a private collector for an exhibition of sixteenth century work. It's a priceless example."

"What does it look like?" Shaley asked.

Gray peered at him closely. "You never saw the *Red Goose?*"

"No," said Shaley patiently. "I never saw the *Red Goose.*"

Gray shook his head pityingly.

Shaley took out his handkerchief and wiped his forehead. "Listen," he said in a strained voice. "Would you mind giving me a description of that picture?"

"Certainly," said Gray quickly. "It's twelve inches by fifteen. It's a reproduction of a pink goose in a pond of green water lilies. A beautiful work."

"It sounds like it," Shaley said sourly. "How was it stolen?"

"It was cut out of the frame with a razor blade. I never heard of such an act of vicious vandalism! They cut a quarter of an inch off the painting all around it!"

"Terrible," Shaley agreed. "When was this done?"

"I told you. Three days ago."

Shaley took a deep breath and let it out very slowly. "I know you told me three days ago," he said in a deceptively mild voice. "But what time of the day was it stolen—at night?"

"Oh, no. In the afternoon."

"Where were your guards?"

"They were stopping the fight."

Shaley made a sudden strangling noise. He took off his hat and dropped it on the floor. He glared at Gray. Gray stared back at him in mild surprise. Shaley picked up his hat and straightened it out carefully.

"The fight," he said, his voice trembling a little. "There was a fight, then?"

"Why, yes," said Gray. "I forgot to mention it. Two men got into a fight in the back gallery, and it took four of the guards to eject them from the premises. And then we noticed that the picture was gone."

"That's fine," Shaley told him sarcastically. "Now would it be too much trouble for you to describe these men who fought?"

Gray said: "I noticed them particularly, because they seemed a trifle out of place in a museum. One was a big, tall man with long arms and short legs. He had four gold teeth, and he was bald, and his ear—" Gray stopped, hunting for the word.

"Cauliflower?" Shaley asked.

Gray nodded quickly. "Yes. Thick and crinkly. The man interested me as an example of arrested development in the evolutionary process."

Shaley blinked. He scratched his head, squinting.

"You mean he looked like an ape?" he asked.

Gray nodded again. "He had certain definite characteristics—the small eyes sunken under very heavy brows, the flattened nose, the abnormally protruding jaw—that have come to be associated with the development of the human race in its earlier stages."

"That's nice," Shaley said blankly. "What did the other one look like?"

"A nice looking young man. A trifle rough-looking—but

quiet and self-effacing. He had red hair and big pink freckles. The thumb on his left hand was missing."

"That's enough," Shaley said. "Have you notified the police of the theft?"

"Oh, no. Mr. Denton advised us not to. He said the thieves might destroy the picture if they thought the police were after them." Gray shook his head sadly at the thought of such an outrage. "Mr. Denton said to tell you to get it back for nothing if you could; but that the museum was willing to pay up to five thousand dollars. The picture must be returned undamaged. It's a matter of honor with the museum. It would be a terrible blow to our reputation if the property of a private collector should be lost while in our possession."

Shaley stood up. "I'll see what I can do."

"Mr. Denton said he would take care of your fee."

Shaley said: "I'll take care of him. Calling me a crook."

SHALEY DROVE HIS battered Chrysler roadster into Hollywood, entered a drug-store and went into one of the telephone booths in back.

He took a leather-covered notebook from his pocket, flipped through the pages, found the number he wanted. He put a nickel in the phone and dialed.

"Yeah?" It was a thin, flat voice.

"This is Ben Shaley, Mike."

"Oh, hello, Ben. Wait a minute." The voice pulled a little away from the telephone. "Turn that radio down. How the hell do you think I can hear?" The voice came closer again. "How are you, Ben? Long time no see."

"I'm okey, Mike. How you doing?"

"Damn' good. I got the place all redecorated. I got a real bar now—a swell one—mahogany. Come on out, sometime, Ben."

"Thanks, Mike. Listen, is that guy that writes for *Ring and Turf* there—Pete Tervalli?"

"Yeah. He's upstairs playin' blackjack. You want him?"

"Uh-huh."

"I'll call him. Hold the phone."

Shaley waited, tapping out a complicated rhythm on the mouth-piece of the telephone and humming softly.

"Hello, Ben. This is Pete Tervalli."

Shaley said: "Pete, I want to ask you about a couple of guys. Number one is a big gook that looks like an ape. He's got gold front teeth, a flat snozzle, a thick ear, and he's bald. Know him?"

"Nope," said Pete. "He's a new one on me."

"All right. Here's the other one. He's red-headed and sort of quiet, and he's got big pink freckles on his face. He's minus his left thumb."

"Sure," said Pete. "Sure. That's Fingers Reed. He fights in prelims at the Legion stadium sometimes. Been on at the Olympic a couple times, too. Had a semi-final down to Venice once—got knocked out."

"Where can I find him?"

"At Pop's gym down on main."

"Thanks a lot, Pete."

SHALEY WENT UP a flight of long, dark stairs littered with white blotches that were ground-out cigarette butts. He went along a short, dirty hall, through swinging double doors with frosted glass panels.

He was in a big high-ceilinged room that smelled strongly of tobacco, liniment, gin and sweat. A youth in a grayish sweat-shirt was jumping rope in the middle of the floor. He skipped expertly and solemnly, first from one foot and then the other, counting aloud. In one corner a punching bag battered back and forth in a stuttering roar under the quick fists of a small, bow-legged Filipino. In another corner a fattish man made a rowing machine creak mournfully.

Shaley walked along the wall and entered an open door. It was a small office with a dusty desk in one corner. The walls were papered with the pictures of fighters in various belligerent poses.

Shaley said: "Hello, Pop," to the man sitting at the desk.

Pop was a small man with a shiny bald head. He wore a celluloid collar so high that it took him just under the ears and made him look like he was always stretching his neck. He had a dead brown-paper cigarette in one corner of his mouth.

"Hello, Ben," he said without enthusiasm.

"Where can I find Fingers Reed?"

"Fingers Reed?" Pop repeated absently. "Fingers Reed? I wouldn't know him. He a fighter?"

Shaley grinned. "Come on, Pop. Don't pull that stuff. I just want to give him twenty bucks. Which one is he?"

"Give me the twenty," Pop requested. "He owes it to me for gym fees. He's in the ring."

Shaley went out of the office, through another door and into a small room with seats in high, close tiers against three of its walls. There was a ring in the middle.

Fingers Reed, in a heavy sweat-shirt and helmet, was sparring with a tall, spider-legged middleweight. The middleweight danced around very fancily, stepping high. Fingers

Reed shuffled after him, his left poked out in front of him, his right held back shoulder high. He was much too slow for the middleweight. He crossed his right again and again—long, heavy blows that the middleweight slipped easily.

A little man in a checkered cap stood beside the ring. He had a watch in one hand and a string in the other. He pulled the string as Shaley watched. The gong boomed.

Fingers Reed and the middleweight patted each other on the back and started walking back and forth in the ring, breathing deeply and swinging their arms.

Shaley said: "Fingers!"

Fingers Reed stopped and looked down at him.

"I want to talk to you a minute," Shaley said.

Fingers Reed nodded. He slid through the ropes, jumped down on the floor. With the thumb of his right boxing glove, he hooked a rubber tooth protector out of his mouth. He spat on the floor and ran his tongue over his front teeth.

"What?"

Shaley said: "Who paid you to put on that fracas at the museum?"

Fingers Reed pulled up the front of his sweat-shirt. He had an inner tube, cut open, wound tightly around his stomach. He loosened the inner tube a little. Then he rubbed his nose with the back of one glove, squinting sidewise at Shaley.

"I had an idea there was something sour about that."

Shaley said: "I don't want to get hard about it, but there was a picture lifted while you were having that little to-do, and I want to know about it."

"Sure," said Fingers. "Somebody tells me that they got some pictures of some old fight scenes over in this museum in Pasadena, and me not having nothing to do, I think I will go over and take a look at them. So I do, and they are pretty good pictures, too. After I am done looking at them I walk around to take a look at the rest of the stuff, and while I am looking up comes this big monkey and steps on my foot." He stopped and nodded at Shaley.

"So what?" said Shaley woodenly.

"Well, so I ask him what the hell he thinks he is doing, dancing with me? And then he hauls off and pops me, so I pop him back, and pretty soon a few guys in monkey suits come along and toss us both out on our ears." Fingers gestured with the boxing gloves. "So that's that."

Shaley said: "You wouldn't know this big monkey's name?"

Fingers shook his head. "Never saw him before or since."

Shaley took a twenty-dollar bill out of his vest pocket and folded it lengthwise and looked at Fingers calculatingly.

"That's too bad," he said regretfully. He poked the twenty back into his vest pocket. "Well, I'll be going, then. Thanks."

"Wait, now," said Fingers. "Wait a minute. Don't get in a rush."

Shaley took the bill out of his pocket and gave it to him.

Fingers said: "Here, Jig. Keep it for me." He tossed the folded bill to the timekeeper.

"Let's have the real dope," Shaley requested.

"Well, it's like this. The big monkey's name is Gorjon. He's the stooge for a gent by the name of Carter. The two of them come around the gym here a couple of times, and then they put this proposition up to me. Would I put on a phoney fight at the museum for ten bucks? I was flat, so I said sure, why not? So I did."

"Where can I get hold of these boys?"

Fingers shrugged. "By me."

Shaley said gently: "You wouldn't try to be smart with me, would you, Fingers? You wouldn't try to shake me down?"

Fingers held up one gloved hand, palm out. "So help me. I never see them but three times."

Shaley said: "It'd be worth a hundred to me if I could locate them."

Fingers blinked thoughtfully, rubbing his nose with the glove on his right hand. "Hm. The big boy is a fight fan. You might stake out the stadiums around here."

"You do it. You might get some of your pals to help. I could make it fifty for the guy that found them and a hundred to you."

Fingers nodded. "Okey."

WHEN SHALEY CAME into his office, Sadie, his secretary, was tapping away briskly on the typewriter with glossy, pink-nailed fingers.

"Hi-yah," said Shaley, tossing his hat on the hat-rack and heading for the inner office.

Sadie raised her sleek, dark head and watched him. She didn't say anything.

Shaley got to the door of the inner office, then turned around and came back to her desk.

"Well, what's your trouble?"

Sadie said: "A woman called you up. Who is she?"

"How do I know who she is? Who'd she say she was?"

Sadie sniffed. "She wouldn't tell me her name. Talked like a blonde though."

"How'd you know she was blonde?"

"Humph! I can tell, all right. Talking baby talk—all about a red goose. Who ever heard of a red goose?"

"Did you get her number?" Shaley demanded.

"Certainly I did. I always remember to ask people their number."

"Hell—Give me that number."

Sadie shoved a pad of paper along the desk. Shaley picked up her telephone and began to dial the number.

"And my mother was saying just last night," said Sadie righteously, "that she didn't think this office was the proper place for a young girl to work. All these questionable people coming in and out all day long and you swearing and yelling at me all the time and—"

"Shut-up," said Shaley absently.

"Hello." It was a nice voice—small and clear and sweet—shyly innocent.

"This is Ben Shaley. Did you call my office?"

The nice voice said: "Oh, yes."

"About the *Red Goose?*"

"Yes, Mr. Shaley. I called the museum, and they told me you were in charge. Are you looking for the picture?"

Shaley said suspiciously: "Who're you? A reporter?"

"Oh, no. I'm the one that has the picture."

Shaley nearly dropped the telephone. "What?"

"Well, Mr. Shaley, I haven't exactly got it right here. But I can get it for you. Do you want it?"

"Where are you?" Shaley demanded. "When can I see you?"

"I'll be home tonight at seven-thirty. It's the Hingle Manor Apartments on Harcourt just south of Sunset, in Hollywood.

Apartment seven. The name is Marjorie Smith."

"I'll be there, Marjorie," Shaley said cheerfully, hanging up.

He put the telephone slowly back on Sadie's desk, frowning thoughtfully. He picked up her pencil and drew a pattern of squares on the desk-pad, still frowning.

"You know," he said absently, "someway or other I didn't like the sound of that. It sounded just a little screwy. I wonder if somebody is trying to lay me an egg?"

"Humph!" said Sadie. "Blondes!"

HINGLE MANOR WAS a long, neat, two-story stucco building with turrets on the four corners and blue pennants on each of the turrets. Floodlights placed on the front lawn and slanted up made the building look larger and newer than it was.

Shaley found the card that said: "Marjorie Smith," and buzzed the bell under it. After a while the latch clicked. Shaley pushed open the door and was in a small, narrow hall, thickly carpeted.

He looked around, then went up a short flight of stairs. At the end of the hall an open door made a yellow square of light that was like a picture frame for the young woman standing there.

Shaley was reminded of an old-fashioned tintype he had once seen in a family album. The woman wore a neat blue dress, modest and plain. She had wide blue eyes and corn-colored hair wound around her small head in thick braids. Given a sun-bonnet and a slate, she would have been a perfect copy of a school girl of fifty years ago.

She smiled and curtsied a little and said shyly: "Won't you come in, please?"

Shaley went into a small, well-furnished living-room and stood there holding his hat in his hands and shifting from one foot to the other uneasily.

The woman came into the room, shutting the door. She sat down on a couch and folded her hands neatly in her lap.

"I'm Marjorie Smith," she said, smiling nicely.

"I'm Ben Shaley."

Marjorie Smith smiled up at him with admiring blue eyes. Shaley watched her uncomfortably. Something was wrong with all this. Marjorie Smith didn't fit in with the rest of the picture—with Fingers Reed and Carter and Gorjon.

"Who lives here with you?" he asked. She shook her head, wide-eyed. "No one."

"Are we here alone?" She nodded. "Oh, yes."

Shaley grunted. He scratched his head, scowling. He said:

"Listen, Marjorie, I'm just a nasty man with mean suspicions. The only kind of fairy stories I believe are the kind they tell about the boys who carry handkerchiefs in their cuffs. Just sit right here while I sniff around."

"Oh, surely," said Marjorie.

He nosed through the rest of the apartment—kitchen, bedroom, bathroom, closets. He shot the bolt on the back door. He came back into the front room, opened the front door, peered out into the hall. He sat down in a chair and stared at Marjorie Smith.

"Well, I'll be damned," he said blankly.

She put her hand up over her mouth. "Why, Mr. Shaley!"

"Excuse me," said Shaley. "But this is over my head like a tent. Let's talk business."

"Oh, yes," said Marjorie Smith. "Oh, yes. Business." She

leaned forward and watched him with big blue eyes.

"You've got the painting I want—the *Red Goose?*"

She nodded earnestly. "Yes."

"Where'd you get it?"

"A man gave it to me—a man by the name of John Jones."

"That was nice of him," Shaley said.

"He said you would pay me two thousand dollars for it."

"He's an optimist," Shaley said sourly. "It seems like a lot of money, doesn't it?" Marjorie Smith asked earnestly. "But John Jones assured me that it was worth that much. Have you got the money, Mr. Shaley?"

"Huh!" said Shaley. "Where's the picture?"

"John Jones said I was not to give it to you until you gave me the money."

"John's a smart fellow," said Shaley. "But I can't give you the money until I know if you have the picture."

"Oh, but I have got it."

"Yes, yes. But I want to see it. Where is it?"

She shook her head regretfully. "Not until you give me the money. Then I'll give it to you. Really I will, Mr. Shaley."

Shaley took a deep breath and held himself in. "Listen, Marjorie, I don't want to get hard with you, but if I were you I'd hand over that picture right now."

"But, Mr. Shaley, I explained—"

"Once more—will you give me that picture?"

"But, Mr. Shaley—"

Shaley jumped for her. He grabbed her by the shoulders and hauled her off the couch and shook her.

"Now, you little dummy—" he snarled.

She made no resistance. Her body was soft and relaxed in

his hands. She moved just enough to bring her right hand up under Shaley's nose.

She held a small bottle in her hand, uncorked.

Shaley got one whiff of the contents of that bottle. He choked suddenly. He let go of Marjorie Smith and jumped backwards, gasping.

"Acid!" he said, one hand over his nose.

"Yes," she said, smiling just as nicely as before. "Touch me again, and I'll throw it in your face."

Shaley swallowed hard. The picture wasn't out of focus any more. Marjorie Smith fitted right in.

"Wow!" said Shaley in an awed voice, backing away from her warily. He backed clear to the door, keeping his eyes on the bottle.

"Now listen, boob," said Marjorie Smith in her clear, child-like voice. "Let me tell you something—"

THE DOOR BEHIND Shaley opened suddenly, bunting him forward. He whirled around, one hand inside his coat, and looked squarely into the blunt, round muzzle of an automatic. His hand came out, empty.

"Take it easy, baby."

Gray had given a good description. This man Gorjon looked like an ape. He had enormously broad, sloping shoulders, hunched forward. He stood there, swaying a little easily. The gold front teeth gleamed as he grinned at Shaley.

Another man was standing in the doorway behind Gorjon. This man didn't look at Shaley. He was looking at Marjorie Smith.

"Double-crossing little tramp," he said levelly.

He stepped around Gorjon and went towards her, walking springily on the balls of his feet. He was short and round and plumply dapper. He had thick red lips and a small black mustache. He wore a soft white felt hat. He was smiling a little.

Marjorie Smith had hidden the hand holding the acid bottle behind her. She watched the fat man. She waited until he put out a plump, white hand, reaching for her, and then she said something to herself in a tight whisper and hurled the acid at him with a quick sweep of her arm.

The fat man was astoundingly quick. He dropped into a crouch, ducking his head. The acid missed him, spattering on the wall in a bubbling brown stain.

The fat man bounced up again instantly and hit her with his fist. Marjorie Smith fell over a chair and lit on her hands and knees in the corner.

Gorjon hadn't moved either his eyes or the automatic from Shaley. He reached out one big hand and shut the door.

"Sit down, mister," he said to Shaley.

Shaley sat down slowly and tensely in the chair in back of him.

The fat man picked up Marjorie Smith effortlessly and planked her down on the couch. He was still smiling.

She didn't say anything. She watched the fat man expressionlessly. There was a red mark on her face where he had hit her.

The fat man turned to Gorjon. "Take his gun."

Gorjon reached inside Shaley's coat and pulled out the big automatic Shaley carried in a shoulder-holster. He hefted it, grinning.

"It's a .45. He goes loaded for bear. Maybe he's one of these here rough characters you read about in the papers."

The fat man said: "Who is he, Marj?"

Marjorie Smith said sullenly: "Ben Shaley. He's a private peeper—from the museum."

Shaley said: "And you are Carter."

The fat man smiled at him. "So you found Reed, did you? I knew that dead-head would blab all he knew. Yeah, Carter is one of my names. Take a good look at me. Me and Gorjon are gonna be your shadows until you get that money from the museum." He turned back to Marjorie Smith. "Where's the picture?"

"Try and find it."

Carter said: "I will," softly.

He picked her up by the front of her dress and slapped her in the face—quick, sharp slaps that rocked her head back and forth.

"Hey!" said Shaley.

Gorjon pushed his automatic into Shaley's neck. "I wouldn't poke my head out, boy."

Carter said: "Well?" and stopped slapping Marjorie Smith.

She spat at him. He hit her in the mouth with his fist and knocked her back on the couch.

"Rap that boob on the nut," he said calmly to Gorjon, "and take her shoes off. We'll have to get rough with her."

Marjorie Smith wiped her mouth with the back of her hand. Her lips left a little smear of blood on her hand.

"I'll tell you," she said thickly. "Tannerwell has it."

Carter watched her thoughtfully. "Tannerwell, huh? You wouldn't fool an old Civil War vet, would you, Marj?"

"Tannerwell has it."

Carter moved his plump shoulders. "So it was that artist sap, huh? I didn't think he had it in him. Where is he?"

"I don't know."

Carter said very gently: "Where is he, Marj?"

She shrugged impatiently. "I tell you I don't know. I've got his telephone number. I can get him to come here."

"That's just dandy," said Carter. "What's the number?"

"Rochester 2585."

Carter went over to the stand near the door and picked up the telephone. "I'll talk to him first, and then I'll let you. You tell him to come over here—and make it good. I'm going to be mad if you try something funny."

Marjorie Smith said: "He'll come."

Carter dialed the number. He waited, listening. Then he said:

"Hello, Tannerwell? This is Carter." He listened, grinning at Shaley. Then he said: "Yes. Your dear old pal, Carter. Now listen, smarty, while I tell you something. I'm over at Marj's apartment. You get that picture and come over here, or something sudden will happen to her. She's going to talk to you."

He held the mouthpiece of the telephone in front of Marjorie Smith.

She said brokenly: "Bill—Bill. Come quick. Bring the picture." Then she screamed suddenly, so loudly it made Shaley jump.

Carter pushed down the receiver hook with his thumb and put the telephone back on its stand. "Dandy, Marj. You should go on the radio."

"He'll be here in about fifteen minutes," Marjorie Smith said, still sullen.

Carter pulled up a chair and sat down. He tipped his hat back and began to whistle softly and patiently between his teeth, watching Marjorie Smith unblinkingly. Gorjon stood just behind Shaley's chair.

Shaley said: "How about sitting down? You make me nervous."

Gorjon chuckled. "Don't get too nervous, because if you start jiggling around this thing is liable to go off."

"Do you think you're going to put this over?" Shaley asked Carter.

Carter stopped whistling long enough to say: "I think so," and then began again. He stopped and looked at Shaley. "Just keep your nose out of this, baby. When I get that picture, then you and me will have a little talk. Until then you're just a kibitzer. Don't get the idea that anybody has dealt you a hand."

Marjorie Smith moved impatiently on the couch. "Can I have a cigarette?"

Carter said: "I don't smoke, dearie. You know that."

"There's some cigarettes in my right-hand coat pocket," Shaley said.

Gorjon fished the package out and tossed it on the couch.

Marjorie Smith took one and used the lighter on the table at the end of the couch.

Carter got up and turned on the radio. He found a dance orchestra, nodded approvingly, sat down, and began to whistle in tune with it, tapping his foot.

They waited.

IT TOOK TANNERWELL sixteen minutes. His footsteps came up the hall noisily, running. He rapped loudly on the door.

Carter got up quickly and got against the wall beside the

door. He nodded at Marjorie Smith.

She said: "Come in, Bill."

Tannerwell came in with a rush. Carter pushed the door shut behind him.

Tannerwell didn't pay any attention to him. He went straight to Marjorie Smith and stood over her anxiously.

He didn't look like an artist. He looked more like a football player. He was tall, and he had wide, square shoulders. He was blond, and his features were evenly handsome, except for his nose, which had been broken and set crookedly.

"You screamed," he said to Marjorie Smith.

She sniffed a little, sadly. "D-did you bring the pic-picture, Bill?" She looked woe-begone and bedraggled. She looked like a hurt child, crying there on the couch.

Tannerwell jerked a roll of parchment from inside his coat. "Sure. Here." He tossed it over his shoulder at Carter. He never took his eyes from Marjorie Smith.

Carter unrolled the parchment and examined it approvingly.

"Well," he said pleasantly. "Here we are at last."

"Marjorie," Tannerwell said. "Over the telephone. You screamed. Did they hurt you?" He put his hands out in front of him. He had big hands with long, thick fingers. He moved the fingers a little. "Did they hurt you, Marjorie?"

She sobbed. "Y-yes. Look." She pulled aside the neck of her dress and showed a round, ugly burn on the white skin of her shoulder. "Carter burned me with a cigarette to make me scream. He laughed when he did it."

Carter looked up from the picture. "Here!" he said, blankly amazed. "What—"

Tannerwell stared at the burn on Marjorie Smith's shoulder.

Suddenly his face twisted crazily. He spun around and grabbed Carter by the neck with both big hands.

"Hey!" Said Gorjon, starting around in front of Shaley.

Shaley braced his arms on the chair and kicked him savagely in the stomach with both feet. Gorjon doubled over, grunting.

Shaley jumped out of the chair. He got hold of the barrel of the automatic and twisted it out of Gorjon's hand.

Gorjon straightened up. He was grinning. He hit Shaley's wrist with the edge of one palm and knocked the automatic on the floor. He reached for Shaley.

Shaley swung on him with both fists, backing away. He hit Gorjon five times as hard as he could, squarely in the face. Gorjon shook his head, still grinning. He shuffled after Shaley, reaching.

Shaley hit him some more. It was like pounding on a wall. Gorjon didn't even try to block the blows. He let Shaley hit him. He even chuckled a little, his gold teeth gleaming. He was like a cat playing with a mouse. He had forgotten all about Carter and Tannerwell. He kept shuffling after Shaley, one hunched shoulder pushed forward, sidling a little.

Shaley bumped into a chair, and Gorjon got him. He got one big hand in the front of Shaley's coat. He pulled him forward and hit him with the other hand.

Shaley's coat ripped, and he went backward. He bounced off the table, fell over a chair. He got up quickly. He was breathing in gasping sobs. Over Gorjon's shoulder he caught a quick glimpse of the rest of the room and realized that all this was happening in seconds instead of hours.

Tannerwell was still shaking Carter by the neck. Carter's plump face was beginning to turn purple. He was trying to get a revolver from his pocket, but apparently the sight had caught in the cloth and, with Tannerwell shaking him, he couldn't get it free.

Marjorie Smith was still sitting on the couch. And she was laughing. She was laughing at Carter, pointing her finger mockingly at him.

Shaley slipped along the wall away from Gorjon's reaching hands. Gorjon got too close, and Shaley began to hit him again, putting everything he had in each blow. Gorjon grinned and shuffled after him.

Shaley tripped over a stool and fell. Gorjon dropped on him. He got Shaley by the neck, loosely, and began to pound his head on the floor slowly and methodically, chuckling gleefully to himself.

The room rocked in front of Shaley in a red haze. His fingers scrabbled on the floor, touched the barrel of Gorjon's automatic. He twisted and squirmed, scraping at the automatic with stiff fingers.

The red haze began to get black slowly. Gorjon's face was a long way above him—like a gleaming pin-point that nodded and bobbed and leered.

Shaley got his stiff fingers around the butt of the automatic, pushed the muzzle against Gorjon's side.

At its blasting report the room suddenly cleared in front of Shaley's eyes. Gorjon fell over sidewise, very slowly, and hit the floor and lay there without moving.

Shaley got slowly to his feet, staggering a little. His nose was broken. He could feel the blood running down his face. He started towards Tannerwell and Carter.

Carter saw him coming and finally got his pistol free. He

slapped Tannerwell on the side of the head with it. Tannerwell dropped him and bent over, holding his head.

Carter took a quick snap shot at Marjorie Smith that pocked the plaster just above her head. Then he whirled and ducked towards the door. He still held the roll of parchment in his left hand.

Shaley dived for him. He hit Carter's knees just as Carter was going through the door. They rolled out into the hall.

Carter was amazingly strong and quick. It was like trying to hold a squirming ball of soft rubber. He got one leg loose, kicked Shaley in the face. He hit Shaley's broken nose, and Shaley writhed on the floor, swearing thickly, losing his grip on Carter's legs.

Carter bounced to his feet instantly. He ran down the hall towards the stairs.

"Carter!"

It was Marjorie Smith. She was standing in the doorway, and she had the .45 automatic Gorjon had taken from Shaley in one small hand.

Carter whirled around like a dancer and jumped sidewise crouching. Marjorie Smith shot him.

The bullet caught Carter and slammed him back and down in a limp pile. His arms and legs moved aimlessly. After a second he got slowly to his feet and staggered down the hall.

Marjorie Smith shot him again, deliberately, in the back. Carter collapsed weakly and slid down the stairs, bumping soddenly on each step.

A woman was screaming somewhere close by. Shaley got up off the floor. He walked down the hall, guiding himself with one hand on the wall and trying to keep his feet from walking out from under him. He got to Carter and leaned over to pick up the picture. He fell down and got up again slowly, holding the picture.

Marjorie Smith came running down the hall. She was pulling Tannerwell along behind her. She looked calm, sure of herself, as if she knew just where she was going. Tannerwell was shaking his head foggily, and he staggered a little as he ran.

They went by Shaley without even looking at him.

Feet were pounding up and down the hall overhead. A half dozen people were screaming for the police into telephones and out windows.

Shaley climbed the stairs, shuffled slowly towards the rear entrance.

A man opened a door, looked at him blankly, said: "Good God! He's all blood!" and slammed the door.

Shaley got out the back door into cool darkness. He fell over a hedge, got up, and ran heavily through a weed-choked lot, swearing to himself in a mumbling monotone. A siren began to moan in the distance.

SHALEY HAD A piece of white court-plaster over his nose. It made his tanned face look darker and thinner. He had his hat tipped forward over his face because the back of his head was swollen.

He walked down a long, gloomy hall and found Gray at the end of it. Gray was on top of a high step-ladder carefully dusting a painting with a brush about an inch wide. He dusted in quick, dabbing strokes, stopping every minute to squint sidewise at the picture through his thick, dusty glasses.

Shaley said: "Hello!"

Gray said: "How do you do, Mr. Shaley," without looking around.

Shaley leaned against the brass railing and watched him. "Well," he said. "It's a long story. Want to hear it?"

Gray dabbed busily at the picture. "Certainly, Mr. Shaley."

"A guy by the name of Carter stole the picture. The fight was staged by a pal of his and another bird they had hired, to attract the guards' attention while Carter got the picture. Carter had spotted this scatter as an easy one to crack, but he didn't know anything about pictures. So he hired an artist to pick out the right one to steal. The artist selected the *Red Goose.*"

Gray nodded. "A good choice, I must say. It's a very beautiful painting."

"Carter didn't care whether it was beautiful or not. He wanted something the museum would want back in a hurry—something that couldn't be replaced. So he took the *Red Goose.* But Carter had a girl by the name of Marjorie Smith. The artist fell for her. She got ideas. She stole the picture from Carter and lit out with it and the artist. She got in touch with me, intending to sell me the picture for the museum. But Carter found her, just about that time. Are you listening?"

"Yes, yes," said Gray absently. "Go on."

"The artist had the picture. Carter had Marjorie Smith. She pulled a fake screaming act over the telephone to get the artist to bring the picture to Carter. Then, when the artist got there, she double-crossed Carter again. She told the artist that Carter had actually tortured her to make her scream over the telephone. She had burned herself with a cigarette to make it look better. The artist is nuts about her, and he went screwy and tackled Carter. Carter and his pal got themselves killed in the excitement, and I got a broken nose, and Marjorie and her friend Tannerwell got away."

"Tannerwell," said Gray thoughtfully. "Tannerwell. Oh, yes! He's the man that brought back the picture."

There was a long silence.

At last Shaley said: "Brought back—the picture?" in a strained voice.

Gray looked down at him. "Oh, yes. I must have forgotten to notify you. A man by the name of Tannerwell came around yesterday afternoon some time after you left. He had the *Red Goose,* and I paid him three thousand dollars for it. We had promised not to ask any questions about how he happened to have it—we only wanted the picture back."

Shaley took the roll of parchment from his coat pocket with fumbling fingers. "What's this, then?"

Gray trotted down the step-ladder. He examined the picture, holding it up to the light and nodding in a pleased way to himself.

"Yes. Nice work. Of course it hasn't the depth, the color blending of the original, but it's very nice work."

Shaley said thickly: "It's—it's a copy?"

"Oh, yes. Couldn't you see that? Mr. Tannerwell told me, after it came into his hands he had made a copy of the picture to keep for himself."

Shaley said: "That little tramp. She had Tannerwell copy the painting intending to shake me down with it. Then when Carter butted in, she just switched her plans a little."

Gray smiled at him. "I'm sorry you were deceived, Mr. Shaley. You could say that the *Red Goose* was a sort of red herring, couldn't you?"

"I could say a lot worse than that," said Shaley.

The Price of a Dime

It was an old trick but this time it started fireworks

SHALEY WAS SITTING behind the big desk in his private office. He had his hat on, pushed down over his forehead, so that the wide brim shaded his hard, narrowed eyes, his thin, straight nose. He had an opened penknife in his hand, and he was stabbing the soft wood of a drawer of the desk in an irritated way.

There was a sudden shrill scream from the outer office.

Shaley started. He scowled at the door.

In the outer office a chair tipped over with a crash. There was another scream, louder than the first one.

Shaley tossed his penknife on the desk and got up.

"She'll drive me crazy one of these days," he muttered, heading for the door in long-legged strides.

He banged the door open, looked through into the outer office.

Sadie, his secretary, was scuffling with a fattish blonde woman. Sadie had the woman by the shoulders, trying to push her through the door into the corridor. The blonde woman's face was puffy, tear-stained. She had a desperately hopeless expression. She was the one who was doing the screaming.

Sadie had her sleek, dark head down, pushing determinedly, but the blonde woman's weight was too much for her.

Shaley said: "Well?" in an explosively angry voice.

Both women turned on him. Sadie got started first.

"You told me you didn't want to see anybody this morning, and she wanted to see you, and I told her you couldn't see her, and she wouldn't go away, and so I tried to put her out, and she started to scream." Sadie said this all in one breath.

The blonde woman sniffed a little. "I've got to see you. I've got to see you, Mr. Shaley. It's about Bennie. I've got to see you."

"All right, all right," Shaley said helplessly. "All *right!* Come on in here."

"But you told me—" Sadie protested.

"Will you kindly sit down and get to work?" Shaley asked in an elaborately courteous voice.

Sadie blinked. "Yes, Mr. Shaley," she said meekly.

Shaley jerked his head at the blonde woman. "Come in." He shut the door of the private office again, pointed to a chair. "Sit down." He walked around his desk, sat down in his chair, and dropped his hat on the floor beside him. He frowned at the blonde woman. "Now what is it?"

She was dabbing at her puffy eyes with a handkerchief that was a moist, wadded ball. "I'm sorry I screamed and acted that way, Mr. Shaley, but I had to see you. Bennie told me to see you, and he's in bad trouble, and so I *had* to see you."

"Who's Bennie?"

The blonde woman looked surprised. "He's my brother."

"That makes it all clear," said Shaley. "Does he have a last name?"

"Oh, sure. Bennie Petersen." The blonde woman looked like she was going to start to cry again. "He told me you knew him. He told me you'd help him. He's a bellboy at the *Grover Hotel*"

"Oh," said Shaley understandingly. "Bennie Peterson, huh? That little chiseler—" He coughed. "That is to say, yes. I remember him. What's he done now?"

"The blonde woman sniffed. "It wasn't his fault, Mr. Shaley."

"No," said Shaley. "Of course not. It never is his fault. What did he do?"

"He just lost a dime, Mr. Shaley. And now Mr. Van Bilbo is going to have him arrested."

Shaley sat up straight with a jerk. "Van Bilbo, the movie director?"

She nodded. "Yes."

"Van Bilbo is going to have Bennie arrested because Bennie lost a dime?"

"Yes."

"Hmm," Shaley said, scowling. "Now let's get this straight. Start at the beginning and tell me just what happened—or what Bennie told you happened."

"Well, Bennie took some ginger ale up to a party on the seventh floor of the hotel. This party tipped him a dime. Bennie was coming back down the hall to the elevator. He had the dime in his hand, and he was flipping it up in the air like George Raft does in the movies. But Bennie dropped the dime on the floor. He was just leaning over to pick it up when Mr. Van Bilbo came out of one of the rooms and saw him, and now he's going to have Bennie arrested."

Shaley leaned back in his chair. "So," he said quietly. "The old dropped dime gag. Bennie dropped a dime in front of a keyhole, and he was looking through the keyhole for the dime, when Van Bilbo caught him at it, huh?"

She shook her head. "Oh, no! Bennie wouldn't look through a keyhole. He wouldn't do a thing like that, Mr. Shaley. Bennie's a good boy. Our folks died when we were young, and I raised him, and I know."

Shaley studied her calculatingly. She really believed what she was saying. She really believed that Bennie was a good boy.

"All right," Shaley said gently, smiling at her. "Forget what I said. Of course Bennie wouldn't peek through a keyhole. What did he tell you to say to me?"

"He told me to tell you to go to Mr. Van Bilbo and tell him that it was all right. That Bennie was Mr. Van Bilbo's friend, and that they could get together on this matter and fix it all up. Bennie said you'd understand."

Shaley nodded slowly. "Oh, yes," he said meaningly. "I understand all right. Where is Bennie now?"

"He's hiding so the police won't find him. He told me not to tell anybody where he was."

Shaley smiled at her. "I can't help him unless I know where he is."

"Well ..." Her voice broke a little. "You *are* his friend, aren't you, Mr. Shaley? You *will help* him, won't you? Just this time, Mr. Shaley, please. He promised me he'd never get into trouble again." She stared at him anxiously.

"I'll help him," Shaley said.

She sighed, relieved. "He's hiding in a boarding-house. I don't know the street address, but you can easily find it. It's a big white house with a hedge around it, and it's right in back of the Imperial Theater in Hollywood. He's going by the name of Bennie Smith."

"I'll find him," said Shaley. "Where can I get hold of you?"

"I work in *Zeke's Tamale Shop*. On Cahuenga, north of Sunset."

"I know the place," said Shaley, standing up. He went over and opened the door. "Don't worry about it any more. I'll fix things up for you."

She fumbled with the worn bag she was carrying. "I drew my money out of the bank this morning, Mr. Shaley. I can pay you. I'll pay you right now."

"Forget it," Shaley said, uncomfortably. "I'll send you a bill. And don't give Bennie any of that money. I'll take care of him."

HE STOOD IN the doorway and watched her go through the outer office and out the door into the corridor.

Sadie looked over one slim shoulder at him, with a slight hurt expression.

"I heard what you said to her," she stated, nodding her sleek head. "And you told me just this morning that you weren't going to take any more customers unless they paid you in advance."

"Phooey!" said Shaley. He slammed the door shut and went back and sat down behind his desk.

He picked up the penknife and stared at it thoughtfully.

"I'll fix him up, all right," he said sourly to himself. "I'll wring the little cuss' neck. Picking me to be the stooge in a black-mailing squeeze."

He began to stab the drawer again with the penknife, scowling.

Suddenly the penknife stopped in mid air. Shaley sat still for several seconds, his eyes slowly widening.

He said: "My gawd!" in a thoughtfully awed voice. He sat there for a while longer and then yelled: "Sadie!"

Sadie opened the door and looked in. "What?"

"Listen, there was a murder in some hotel around here about a week back—some woman got herself killed. What hotel was it?"

"The *Grover*," said Sadie.

Shaley leaned back in his chair. He smiled—a hard, tight smile that put deep lines around his mouth. He said: "So," in a quietly triumphant voice.

"I read all about it in the paper," said Sadie. "The woman's name was 'Big Cee.' She was mixed up with some gangsters or something in Cleveland, and the police thought she came out here to hide, and that some of the gangsters found her. The papers said there were no clues to the murderer's identity. Mr. Van Bilbo, the movie director, read about her death, and he felt sorry for her, and he paid for her funeral. I think that was very nice of him, don't you, Mr. Shaley? A woman he didn't know at all, that way."

"Yes," said Shaley. "It was very nice of Mr. Van Bilbo. Go away now. I want to think."

Sadie slammed the door. Shaley picked his hat up off the floor and put it on, tipping it down over his eyes. He slid down in his chair and folded his hands across his chest.

After about ten minutes, he reached out and took up the telephone on his desk and dialed a number.

A feminine voice said liltingly: "This is the *Grover*—the largest and finest hotel west of the Mississippi."

Shaley said: "Is McFane there?"

"Yes, sir. Just a moment, sir, and I'll connect you with Mr. McFane."

Shaley waited, tapping his fingers on the desk top.

"Hello." It was a smoothly cordial voice.

Shaley said: "McFane? This is Ben Shaley."

"Hello there, Ben. How's the private detecting?"

"Just fair. Listen, McFane, have you got a bellhop around there by the name of Bennie Petersen?"

"We did have. The little chiseler quit us last week without any notice at all. Just didn't show up for work. He in trouble?"

Shaley said: "No. Uh-huh. I was just wondering. He quit right after that murder you had, didn't he?"

"Yes, come to think—" McFane stopped short. "Hey! Are you digging on that?"

"No, no," Shaley said quickly. "I was just wondering, that's all."

"Listen, Ben," McFane said in a worried tone. "Lay off, will you? We spent a thousand dollars' worth of advertising killing that in the papers. It gives the hotel a bad name."

"You got it all wrong," Shaley said soothingly. "I'm not interested at all. I was just wondering. So long, McFane, and thanks."

"Wait, Ben. Listen, I'll make it worth your while—I'll retain—"

Shaley hung up the receiver. He walked quickly out of the private office.

"If a guy by the name of McFane calls," he said to Sadie, "tell him I just left for Europe. I'll call you in an hour."

"From Europe?" Sadie asked innocently.

Shaley went out and slammed the door.

THE HIGH BOARD fence had once been painted a very bright shade of yellow, but now the paint was old and faded and streaked. It was peeling off in big patches that showed bare, brown board underneath.

Shaley parked his battered Chrysler roadster around the corner and walked back along the fence. There was a group of Indians standing in a silent, motionless circle in front of the big iron gate. They all had their arms folded across their chests. They all wore very gaudy shirts, and two of the older ones had strips of buckskin with beads sewn on them tied around their heads.

They didn't look at Shaley, didn't pay any attention to him.

Shaley walked up to the iron gate and peered through the thick, rusted bars. There was a car—a yellow Rolls-Royce—parked in the graveled roadway. The hood was pushed up, and two men were listening to the engine.

"If that's what you call a piston slap," one said, "you should be chauffeuring a wheelbarrow."

Shaley said: "Hey, Mandy."

The man straightened, turned around. He was short, dumpy. He was wearing golf knickers and a checked sweater and checked golf hose and a checked cap. He had a round, reddish face sprinkled with brown spots. He was chewing on the stub of a cigar, and tobacco juice had left a brown trail from the corner of his mouth down his chin. He stared at Shaley without any sign of recognition.

"Let me in, Mandy," Shaley requested.

Mandy strolled up to the gate, looked at Shaley through it.

"I don't suppose you'd have a pass, would you?"

Shaley said: "Come on, Mandy. Let me in. I want to talk to you."

"Huh!" said Mandy. He opened the gate grudgingly.

Shaley slipped inside, and Mandy slammed the gate with a clang.

"Go ahead and talk," he invited. "It won't do you any good. I won't buy anything."

Shaley looked at the other man meaningly. This one wore a plum-colored military uniform with silver trimmings. He looked as a motion picture director's chauffeur should look. He was thin and tall with a swarthily dark face and a small black mustache. He had his military cap tipped at a jaunty angle.

He stared from Mandy to Shaley, then shrugged his thin shoulders.

"Excuse me," he said. He slammed the hood down and got into the front seat of the Rolls and backed it up the road.

"Pretty fancy," Shaley said, jerking his head to indicate the chauffeur and the car.

"He gripes me," Mandy said sourly. "I liked old Munn better."

"Why all the war-whoops outside?" Shaley asked.

"Extras. Waitin' to be put on. We ain't gonna shoot any exteriors today. We're shootin' a saloon scene. I told 'em that six times, but you can't argue with them guys. They just grunt at you."

"How's Van Bilbo coming since he's been producing independent?"

Mandy shrugged. "Just fair, I think we got a good one this time—forty-niner stuff."

They were silent, watching each other warily.

Shaley said suddenly: "Who was Big Cee, Mandy?"

"Huh?" Mandy said vacantly.

Shaley didn't say anything. He squatted down on his heels and began to draw patterns in the dust with his forefinger.

After a while, Mandy said bitterly: "I mighta known you'd get on to that. You find out everything, damn you."

There was another silence. Shaley kept on drawing his patterns in the dust.

"Her name was Rosa Lee once," Mandy said sullenly. "She worked with the old man on some serials way back in '09 or '10."

Shaley drew in a long breath. "So," he said quietly. He stood up. "Thanks, Mandy."

"Don't you try any of your sharp-shooting on the old man!" Mandy warned ferociously. "Damn you, Shaley, I'll kill you if you do!"

Shaley grinned. "So long, Mandy." He opened the gate and slipped outside.

Mandy put his head through the bars. "I mean it now, Shaley. You try anything funny on Van Bilbo, and I'll kill you deader than hell!"

SHALEY WENT INTO a drug-store on Sunset and called his office.

"Anybody call me?" he asked, when Sadie answered the telephone.

She said: "Yes, Mr. Shaley. That man McFane called three times. He seems to be mad at you. He swore something terrible when I told him you'd gone to Europe. And that woman called—that woman that was here this morning and didn't pay you any money."

"What'd she want?"

"She wanted to thank you for getting Bennie that job in Phoenix."

"For what?" Shaley barked.

"For getting Bennie that job in Phoenix."

"Tell me just what she said," Shaley ordered tensely.

"She called just a little while ago. She said she wanted to thank you. She said the man you had talked to had called her up and told her that he would give Bennie a job in a hotel in Phoenix, and that she had told the man where Bennie was so the man could go and see him about the job."

Shaley stood there stiffly, staring at the telephone box.

"Hello?" said Sadie inquiringly.

Shaley slowly hung up the receiver, scowling in a puzzled way.

"Good gawd!" he said to himself suddenly in a tight whisper.

He banged open the door of the telephone booth and ran headlong out of the drug-store.

SHALEY PARKED THE Chrysler with a screech of rubber on cement. He got out and walked hurriedly along the sidewalk, along a high green hedge, to a sagging gate. He strode up an uneven brick wall, up steps into a high, old-fashioned porch.

A fat man in a pink shirt was sitting in an old rocker on the porch with his feet up on the railing.

"Where's Bennie Smith's room?" Shaley asked him abruptly.

"Who?"

"Bennie Smith?"

"What's his name?" the fat man inquired innocently.

Shaley hooked the toe of his right foot under the fat man's legs and heaved up. The fat man gave a frightened squawk and went over backwards, chair and all. He rolled over and got up on his hands and knees, gaping blankly at Shaley.

Shaley leaned over him. "Where's Bennie Smith's room?"

"Upstairs," the fat man blurted quickly. "Clear back. Last door on the left." He wiped his nose with the back of his hand. "Gee, guy, no need to get so hard about it. I'd 'a' told you. I was only fooling. No need to get so rough with a fellow."

Shaley was running across the porch. He went in the front door into a dim, moist-smelling hall with a worn green rug on the floor. He went up a flight of dark, carpeted stairs, along a hall.

The last few steps he ran on his toes, silently. He had his hand inside his coat on the butt of the big .45 automatic in his shoulder-holster.

He stopped in front of the last door on the left, listening. He pulled out the automatic and held it in his hand. He knocked softly on the door with his other hand.

There was no answer.

Shaley said: "Bennie," and knocked on the door again.

He turned the knob. The door was locked.

Working silently, Shaley took a ring of skeleton keys out of his left-hand coat pocket. The lock was old and loose. The first key turned it.

Shaley pushed the door open cautiously, standing to one side.

He drew in his breath with a hissing sound.

Bennie was lying on the bed. He looked very small and thin and young. In death his face had lost some of its sharpness, its wise-guy cynicism.

He had been stabbed several times in his thin chest. The bed was messy.

Shaley shut the door very quietly.

SHALEY TURNED OFF of Sunset and drove up Cahuenga. He parked the Chrysler and walked slowly across a vacant lot towards a long, shacklike building that had a big red Neon sign on top of it that said: *Zeke's*.

Shaley walked around to the back and knocked on the door.

An angry voice from inside said: "How many times must I tell you bums that I can't give you no hand-outs until after the rush—" The man opened the door and saw Shaley. He said: "Oh! Hello, Mr. Shaley." He was a short, fat man with a round face that was shiny with perspiration. He wore a white chef's cap.

Shaley craned his neck, peering in the door. He could see into the interior of the dining-car. Bennie's sister was standing at the cash register, joking with a policeman and a man in a bus driver's uniform.

"What's the matter, Mr. Shaley?" the short man asked.

Shaley nodded his head to indicate the blonde woman. "Her brother has just been murdered."

The short man said: "Bennie?"

"Yes."

"Oh, ——!" said the short man. "And she thought he was the grandest thing that ever lived."

"You'll have to tell her," Shaley said.

"Me? Oh, —— no! No. I don't want to. You tell her, Mr. Shaley."

Shaley said: "I can't."

The short man stared at him. "I got to tell her. And she thought he was so swell. She gave him most of her wages." He rubbed his hand across his mouth. "Oh, ——! That poor kid."

Shaley turned around and walked away. He was swallowing hard.

WHEN SHALEY CAME up and peered through the big iron gate, Mandy and the chauffeur were looking into the engine of the Rolls-Royce much in the same attitude as before.

"It's a wrist-pin," Mandy said. "I'm telling you it's a wrist-pin."

Shaley said: "Mandy."

Mandy came over and opened the gate. "You're like a depression," he told Shaley sourly. "Always popping up when people don't expect you. What do you want now?"

"I want to see Van Bilbo."

"He's in his office. They're just gettin' ready for some re-takes on that saloon scene. What's the matter with you, anyway?"

Shaley said: "I just saw a kid that was murdered. He was a little rat and a chiseler and a liar, but he had a swell sister. She trusted me, and I let her down. I'm going to talk to Van Bilbo and then I'm going to start something. Stick around."

He walked along the road, his feet crunching in the gravel.

The chauffeur looked at Mandy. "Screwy?" he inquired.

Mandy was squinting at Shaley back. He shook his head slowly.

"No. He gets that way when he's mad. And when he's mad, he's a great big dose of bad medicine for somebody."

Shaley turned around the corner of a barnlike building and was in a short dusty street with false-fronted sets on each side. There were board sidewalks and a couple of big tents that had saloon signs in front of them.

There were saddled horses tied to a long hitching-rack. There were men in fringed buckskin suits with coonskin caps and long rifles, and men in big sombreros wearing jingling spurs on their boots and big six-shooters in holsters at their waists, and men clad in black with high stovepipe hats. There were girls in low-necked dresses, and girls in calico and sun-bonnets.

A man up on a wooden tower that held an arc lamp was yelling angrily at a man on the ground, who was yelling back at him just as angrily. Two carpenters were having a loud argument in front of a saloon door. Another man had a long list in his hand and was running around checking up on the costumes of the extras. At the side of the street three men had a camera apart, examining its interior gravely.

Shaley walked along the middle of the street, went into a small wooden office building at the far end. He walked down a dusty corridor, knocked on a door that had a frosted glass panel with a crack in it running diagonally from corner to corner.

A voice said: "Come in."

Shaley opened the door and went into a small, cubby-hole of an office.

Van Bilbo was sitting behind the desk. Van Bilbo was a small, thin man. He was bald, and he wore big horn-rimmed glasses that gave him an owlish look. He always reminded Shaley of a small boy making believe he was grown up.

"Hello," he said shyly, peering over his glasses at Shaley.

"Do you remember me?" Shaley asked.

Van Bilbo shook his head, embarrassed. "I'm sorry. I meet so many people … I don't remember.…"

Shaley shut the door and sat down in a chair. "I'll tell you a story—a true one. One time there was a man who was a racetrack driver. He cracked up badly, and his nerves went haywire. He couldn't drive any more. He came out to Hollywood, hoping to find something to do. He didn't. He went broke. One day he was standing outside a studio. He'd pawned everything he owned but the clothes he wore. He was hungry and sick and pretty much down. While he was standing there a director came along. The director gave that man a ten-dollar bill and told him to go get something to eat. He gave the man a work-slip and let him work as an extra for a month, until he got on his feet again. I was that man, and you were the director. I don't forget things like that."

Van Bilbo made flustered little gestures. "It— it was nothing … I don't even remember.…"

"No," said Shaley. "Of course you don't. You've helped out plenty that were down and out and plenty that were in trouble—like Big Cee."

Van Bilbo repeated: "Big Cee," in a scared voice.

Shaley nodded. "That wasn't very hard to figure out, knowing you. She used to work for you a long time ago. She was in a jam. She called on you to help her out, and you did. She was running a joint in Cleveland. She got in wrong with some politicos, and they closed up her place. She was sore. She got hold of some affidavits that would look mighty bad in a court record. She skipped out here, intending to hide here and shake the boys back in Cleveland down for plenty. But they didn't want to play that way. They sent a guy after her, and he biffed her."

Part of this Shaley knew, and part he was guessing; but he didn't have to guess very much; with what he knew, the rest was fairly obvious.

Van Bilbo was staring at the door with widened eyes. Shaley turned to look.

A shadow showed through the frosted glass—a hunched, listening shadow.

Shaley slid the .45 out of his shoulder-holster and held it on his lap, watching the shadow. He went on talking to Van Bilbo:

"That was what happened and everything would have been closed up now and over with, only you and a bellhop, by the name of Bennie, put your fingers in the pie. Big Cee got scared somebody might be after her, and she called you in and gave you the affidavits to keep for her. Bennie saw you leaving her room, and, being a chiseler by trade, he got the idea that he might shake you down a little. He was curious about Big Cee, and he kept on watching the room. He saw the murderer go in and out. Then when he found out Big Cee had been knocked off, Bennie thought he was on easy street for fair."

Shaley paused, watching the shadow. The shadow was motionless.

"Bennie planned to put the squeeze on both you and the murderer. He made a bad mistake as far as the murderer was concerned. This murderer wasn't the kind of a boy to pay hush money. He's a dopey and a killer. Bennie found that out and went undercover while he tried to get in touch with you through me. The murderer was looking for Bennie. In the first place, Bennie knew too much, and in the second place the murderer didn't want Bennie putting the squeeze on you for fear you'd get scared and turn those affidavits over to the police."

The shadow was moving very slowly, getting closer to the door.

Shaley went on quickly: "The murderer was trailing Bennie's sister, trying to locate Bennie. He trailed the sister to me. He used my name to get the sister to give him Bennie's address. He killed Bennie. But he hasn't got those affidavits yet, and he wants them. He paid your chauffeur to quit, so he could get his job and be close to you without anybody getting suspicious. Come on in, baby!"

THE GLASS PANEL of the door suddenly smashed in. An arm in a plum-colored uniform came through the opening. A thin hand pointed a stubby-barreled revolver at the two men inside.

Shaley kicked his chair over backwards just as the revolver cracked out.

Shaley's big automatic boomed loudly in the small room.

There was the pound of feet going quickly down the hall.

Shaley bounced up, kicked his chair aside, jerked the door open.

The thin form in the plum-colored uniform was just sliding around the corner at the end of the hall. Shaley put his head down and sprinted.

He tore out through the door into the street in time to see the plum-colored uniform whisk through the swinging doors of the saloon.

Extras stared open-mouthed. A man with two heavy six-guns and a fierce-looking mustache was trying to crawl under the board sidewalk. One of the dance-hall girls screamed loudly.

Shaley started across the street. There was a little jet of orange flame from the dimness behind the swinging doors. The crack of the revolver sounded slightly muffled.

The horses tied to the hitching-rack reared and kicked, squealing frantically.

Shaley trotted across the dusty street. He had one hand up to shield his eyes from the glare of the sun. He had his automatic balanced, ready, in the other hand.

He got to the swinging doors, pushed them back.

The place was fixed up as a dance-hall and saloon. There was a long bar and a cleared space for dancing with a raised platform for the fiddler at the far end.

Shaley ducked suddenly, and a bullet from the back window smashed into the wall over his head.

He ran across the room and dived headlong through the window. He saw that he had made a mistake while he was still in mid-air. The man in the plum-colored uniform hadn't run this time. He had decided to make a fight of it. He was crouched under the window.

Shaley tried to turn himself around in the air. He hit the ground on one shoulder and rolled frantically. And as he rolled, he caught a glimpse of a thin, swarthy face staring at him over the barrel of a stubby revolver.

There was a shot from the corner of the building. The man in the plum-colored uniform whirled away from Shaley, snarling.

Mandy was standing there, dumpily short, cigar still clenched in his teeth. He had a big, long-barreled revolver in his hand. As the man in the plum-colored uniform turned, Mandy pointed the revolver and fired again.

The man in the plum-colored uniform shot twice at him, and then Shaley's heavy automatic boomed once.

The man in the plum-colored uniform gave a little gulping cry. He started to run. He ran in a circle and suddenly flopped down full-length. The plum-colored uniform was a huddled, wrinkled heap on the dusty ground.

Shaley got up slowly, wiping dust from his face. Heads began to poke cautiously out of windows, and excited voices shouted questions.

Van Bilbo came running—a small, frantic figure with the horn-rimmed glasses hanging from one ear. He ran up to Mandy, pawed at him.

"Are you hurt? Are you hurt, Mandy?"

Mandy said: "Aw, shut up. You're like an old hen with the pip. Of course I ain't hurt. That guy couldn't shoot worth a damn." He pushed Van Bilbo away.

Shaley said to the people who came crowding around: "This man is a dope fiend. He went crazy and suddenly attacked Mr. Van Bilbo. You can all testify that I shot in self-defense."

Mandy was pushing away through the crowd. Shaley followed him.

"Mandy," Shaley said.

Mandy turned around.

"Give me that gun," Shaley demanded and jerked the revolver out of Mandy's hand.

It was a single-action six-shooter. Shaley opened the loading gate, spun the cylinder. He punched out one of the loaded cartridges and looked at it.

The cartridge had no bullet in it. It was a blank.

"I thought so," said Shaley. "You grabbed this one off one

of the extras. You damn' fool, you stood out there in the open with a gun full of blank cartridges and let that monkey shoot at you, just to give me a chance at him. That's guts, Mandy."

"Aw, nerts," said Mandy uncomfortably. "I just didn't think about it, that's all. He got old Munn's job and I didn't like him anyway."

Shaley glanced over where the whiskered man with the two big six-guns was just appearing from under the board sidewalk.

"There's a guy that thought, all right."

Mandy scowled—

"Oh, them!" He spat disgustedly. "Them heroes of the screen ain't takin' no chances gettin' hurt. It'd spoil their act."

Reform Racket

Dan Stiles kicked the racket out of one reform

BRADFORD WAS FAT and pink and jolly. He waved his arms. He laughed at his own jokes. He talked on and on without pausing, without giving Stiles a chance to say anything, and all the time he was watching Stiles out of small, green eyes that didn't seem to belong to the rest of his face.

Stiles was sitting on the edge of the bed. He was smoking a cigarette and watching the smoke curl up towards his thin, tanned face. His eyes were blankly gray, patiently bored. He waited until he was sure Bradford was through talking. Then he said: "I'm glad to see you," as though he weren't very glad.

Bradford rolled his head on thick shoulders, grinning. "Sure, sure. You're glad to see me. And you're gong to give me a chance to get on the band-wagon because I'm a good friend of yours. Is it my fault those dopes pick my club to go to? Is it my fault the Feds knock the joint over? I'm asking you, is it my fault? Can I fix the Feds? No. But I want to do the right thing by you. You just tell me how much, Danny. You just tell me how much, and we'll get together."

"How much what?" Stiles asked.

Bradford was off again. "Heh, heh, heh. You always were a great joker, Danny. Why, I remember back two years before you left, you was sore at Mossy Brown, and you—"

Stiles said: "How much what?"

"Heh, heh. That's funny, Danny, that's funny. Yes, sir, and I'm a man that appreciates a good joke. I—"

Stiles said patiently: "What do you want, Bradford?"

Bradford was still grinning. "Protection, Danny, protection. I'm a business man. I run three clubs. I run 'em quiet. I want to keep 'em open. Little accidents like happened a month ago ain't my fault, are they, Danny?"

"I can't give you any protection."

Bradford stopped grinning. His voice was high and thin as he said: "Throwing me to the wolves, Danny? Forgot what a good friend of yours I am?"

Stiles moved his shoulders impatiently. "Don't be a fool, Bradford. I don't know what you're talking about. I can't give anyone protection."

All the jolliness went out of Bradford's face. His eyes were thin slits of green in a pink circle. "That's the way it goes, huh? All right, Stiles, you wait. You think you're on top now. Just wait, that's all, just wait."

"Get out," Stiles said in a flatly level voice. He jerked his thumb towards the door. "Get, Bradford. Back to the kindergarten."

Bradford stood up. He stood looking down at his hat, turning the hat over and over in his thick fingers. His flat nostrils moved in and out quickly. "You wait. You think you got things sewed up in this town. You wait. I'll show—"

Stiles stood up, and Bradford went through the door. His feet made flapping noises down the hall. Stiles slowly and carefully closed the door. He sat down on the bed and frowned thoughtfully, looking at the white brick wall across the alley from the hotel.

After a while feet made a little sliding noise in the hall outside the door. Stiles put his hand under the pillow on the bed and waited, watching the door move inward, hesitate, then move again.

RAIMLER CAME IN. He shut the door softly and leaned against it. He was chewing gum, and his false teeth made a clicking noise every time his jaws came together. He watched Stiles' hand—the one that was under the pillow.

"Look out," he said at last. "It'll bite yuh."

Stiles brought his hand out from under the pillow. He was holding a packet of cigarettes. He looked from the cigarettes to Raimler and grinned, showing white teeth against his tanned face.

Raimler nodded. "You're a clever boy, Danny. Some time you'll slip."

Stiles was lighting his cigarette. The flame of the match made his eyes shine dully. "Some time you'll open the wrong door, Raimler. That'll give the police department a chance to take up a collection—an extra one. Still peeking through key-holes and breaking up crap games?"

Raimler's mouth twisted. "Yeah. It's funny, ain't it? Ten years without a promotion. Funny as hell."

Stiles examined the end of his cigarette carefully. "Sorry, Raimler. Didn't mean to hit a soft spot."

Raimler shrugged. "Okey. My time's comin'. Bradford left in a big hurry, didn't he?"

"Well, yes and no. And then again, maybe."

Raimler put his hand on the door knob and watched his hand turn it slowly. "I wouldn't do business with him, Danny. You're smart. You can figure things out. But Bradford's dynamite. It was the raid on his *Forty-five Club* that started the reform crowd off. You try to fix things for him and the whole damn' thing will blow up under you."

Stiles said: "I'm not doing any business with him. He said he wanted protection."

Raimler looked up quickly. "What the hell else would he want? A kiss on each cheek? He needs protection. He knows the organization is going to dump him overboard."

Stiles shrugged and watched the smoke from his cigarette climb straight up towards the ceiling and then break into little ringlets.

Raimler coughed. "Guess I'll be goin', Danny."

Stiles said: "See you later." He watched the door close slowly and kept on staring at it, frowning and chewing on his lower lip.

A narrow shaft of sunlight came in through the window and lit up one side of his face, making it look wolfishly hard.

THE BANK WAS doing a good business. People were writing at the desks, standing in line before the grilled windows.

Stiles pushed his way through the ornate lobby and went into the glass partitioned private office without waiting to be announced. He shut the door and sat down in the big chair across from the flat-topped desk. He put his hat on the floor beside him, crossed his legs carefully, folded his hands, and tipped back a little in the chair.

Georgeson was cramped over the desk, writing furiously, his pen sputtering and scratching across the papers in front of him. He was a tall man with a prominent jaw and a high, sloping forehead. He frowned and his lips moved in time to his writing.

Stiles watched him patiently, his tanned face smoothly impassive. After a while Georgeson's face flushed a little. He kept on writing. Stiles began to whistle through his teeth.

Georgeson put his pen back in its holder slowly and carefully. He put his thin elbows on the desk and leaned forward to glare. He was good at glaring. His forehead screwed into a knot, and his eyebrows came together in a point above his nose. His lips were thin and hard, twisted back from his teeth.

The glare didn't bother Stiles any. He began to move a little in his chair, making it squeak in time to his whistle.

Georgeson said: "I wish you'd stop that."

Stiles stopped whistling, smiled and nodded. "How do you do, Mr. Georgeson?"

"I told you to stay out of this town."

Stiles shrugged indifferently. "I forget so easily."

"What'd you come back for?"

"For about two weeks."

Georgeson lifted his upper lip contemptuously. "A hell of a fine brother-in-law you are! A nice advertisement for me and your sister! A gunman, and a gambler, and a soldier-of-fortune! How much do you want?"

Stiles became very still, very quiet. His voice was quiet. "I don't quite get that last remark."

"How much do you want? Oh, I knew this was coming. I knew you'd be back to shake me down, now that you've got a good chance. Go ahead, name your price."

Stiles stood up slowly, picked up his hat, and put it on. "Georgeson," he said carefully, "You're still a damn' fool."

Georgeson's voice was weary. "Don't try to act virtuous. I knew you'd come around to blackmail me. You picked a good time. I'll have to pay. How much do you want?"

Stiles stared at him for a long time, then suddenly chuckled. "You're quite a joke, Georgeson, only you don't know it. I won't bother either Margaret or you." He opened the door. "Cheerio!"

Georgeson's eyes were a little wider. He licked his lips. "Now listen, Dan, no need to get sore. I'll pay you more than they will. Just name your own price, that's all."

Stiles said cheerfully: "Go to hell."

WHEN STILES CAME out of the bank, a puzzled frown between his eyes, he nearly bumped into Raimler, who was standing on the stone steps rolling a cigarette.

"Following me around?" Stiles asked, "or just going the same places I do?"

Raimler looked up. "Who, me? Oh, I just came to see Georgeson. I'm lookin' for a new job."

Stiles was in the act of lighting a cigarette. The lighted match in his hand stopped in mid-air an inch from the end of the cigarette. After a second Stiles blew on the match and threw it away. His eyes were suddenly flat and shiny; and he was smiling without humor, merely lifting the corners of his mouth.

"Huh!" he said slowly. "Well, you better wait until some other time. He's not feeling well this morning."

Raimler was looking down at his cigarette. He folded the paper over with his thumbs and rolled it back and forth. "Stiles, this means a lot to me. I'm throwing in with you."

Stiles said: "With me? What do you want with me?"

The cigarette paper in Raimler's hands suddenly tore across. His voice was thick. "I've taken the dust for ten years. Now, by —— it's my turn! There's a few people in this damned town I'd like to push around a little!"

"But me, Raimler—how do I fit? How could I help you? When I left here, most of the town had little use for me. I come back—for no special reason—and suddenly everybody wants to be my friend, wants me to help 'em. All except Georgeson, of course. He always thought my being around stunk up his atmosphere. What's the answer to the riddle?"

The plain-clothesman glanced at him quickly, keenly. Then he smiled.

"You're all right, Stiles. Only some of these goofs don't know it and if you don't watch out you'll be in a jam. The answer? Why, Georgeson of course. They're electing him mayor on the reform wave—if he doesn't pull any dumb tricks. He married your sister, didn't he? You've got an in, haven't you—or at least they figure that way."

Stiles gave a long, low whistle. His frown disappeared. He grinned, a hard, bitter grin.

"So that's it."

"Yes, that's it, Stiles. And like I said, I'm throwing in with you. I know, what lots of them don't know, you're a square shooter. But watch Bradford. It was the raid on his club that started the stink, and the organization is going to make him the goat. He knows it. That's why he tried to throw in with you.

When you threw him down he naturally thought you were speaking for Georgeson, too. He'll start something now—against both of you."

"He's nothing but wind."

Raimler looked up quickly. "Don't kid yourself. He'll back up his big talk when he's pushed. Watch yourself."

Stiles said: "I can take care of myself. Georgeson will have to look out for what comes his way."

"Okey. See you later."

Stiles stood on the steps for a while, frowning. He had the answer now. Everything was clear. At a sudden thought, he grinned, his hard, tight grin.

LATE IN THE afternoon Stiles came out of the hotel. He stopped a moment on the steps, whistling to himself… He was wearing a blue suit, and a soft gray hat. He came down the steps and turned to the right, walking briskly.

A tall man appeared in front of him, blocking his way. A tall man with an egg-colored complexion and a derby hat pulled low over his eyes.

"Mr. Stiles?"

The muscles along Stiles' back stiffened a little. "Yes."

The tall man was not looking at him. He was looking over Stiles' shoulder. He was grinning showing bad teeth.

"Here, guess this is for you." He extended a legal-looking paper.

Mechanically Stiles took it. The tall man turned suddenly and moved away.

Stiles looked at the paper. It was blank. The seconds seemed to drag by. The tall man was a slow-motion picture. He was running now, with enormously lengthy strides, dodging, dodging right and left.

Stiles suddenly fell flat on the sidewalk. A clattering, continuous roar blotted out everything. Bullets smashed into the wall over his head, crashed through a plate glass window.

Stiles was rolling across the sidewalk towards steps that led back to the basement of the building. The bullets came down off the wall and followed him, knocking flaky lumps of cement out of the sidewalk. The roar in back of him was endless, deafening. He jolted down stone steps, making his body limp.

The bullets played along the edge of the top step, smashed through the window of the door below. Brass things were falling on the floor somewhere.

Stiles was curled up flat on the steps, one arm over his head. The bullets stopped coming. There was the roar of a motor, a clash of gears. A long-drawn squeal of rubber as the car took a corner at high speed.

Everything was quiet for a moment. Then people commenced to yell.

Stiles stood up. His face was expressionless, but he was breathing quick and hard, and his hands trembled a little as he brushed off his clothes.

A fat man came out of the basement door. He looked at Stiles without seeing him.

"Gunmen!" he said breathlessly. "Gangsters! I seen it all! They was after that guy that run! The bullets came right in my door. See?" He pointed to the smashed glass. "Right in my door. They was after that guy that run. Did you see him?" He ran up the stairs to the sidewalk.

Stiles picked up his hat and put it on carefully. He went up the stairs. The fat man was there, talking.

"See? They came right in my door. Bullets. See? They smashed everything. Right in my door. I was inside. They was after the tall guy that run. I seen it all."

Stiles walked on down the street. He planted one foot carefully in front of the other and tried to keep his knees from jerking when his feet hit the sidewalk. He was breathing more evenly now.

When Stiles came back to the hotel two hours later there was a letter waiting for him. It was in a pale blue envelope addressed in a carefully even backhand script with the t's all crossed at an angle.

Stiles took the letter up to his room and opened it. The paper inside was the same shade of pale blue with a thin, looped-gold edging. The letter said:

Dan:

Please come to see me. I am at the same address.

Margaret.

That was all. Not even "Dear Dan," from a sister he hadn't seen in years.

Stiles looked at the letter for a long time. His face was puzzled, doubtful. Finally he folded the letter up and put it in his pocket.

THE BUTLER OPENED the door and looked at Stiles with a half-annoyed, half-condescending air, his eyebrows raised inquiringly.

Stiles said: "Stiles is the name. Mrs. Georgeson will see me."

The butler's face did not change. He opened the door wider.

Margaret was waiting in the center of what was evidently the drawing-room. It was as though the whole room was a stage arranged to emphasize her beauty, and she knew it. She did not look like Stiles except for her wide gray eyes. Her lips were full and red.

She didn't say anything until the butler had withdrawn. Then she came close to Stiles and put her arms around him.

"Dan," she said in a carefully throaty voice. "Dan!"

Stiles said: "Hello, Margaret." He disengaged himself and sat down on the thinly upholstered couch. "You sent for me," he said, looking around for an ash-tray and finally deciding the bronze cupid holding out cupped-hands was one.

Margaret came to the couch and sat down. She stared at him with widened eyes. "Dan, you've been to see Herbert. He told me. You're angry, aren't you?"

Stiles said: "Oh, hell. That half-wit. He thought I came back to town to shake him down. Offered to pay me to leave."

Margaret watched him for a moment and then laughed carefully. "Herbert is so funny. He is so very particular about his reputation."

Stiles stood up.

Her eyes widened farther. She looked deeply hurt. "But Dan! I wanted to talk to you. I haven't seen you for years. You're not going?"

Stiles said: "Oh, for God's sake, Margaret! I don't need a chart. These impossible relatives are always creating embarrassing situations, aren't they?"

Margaret said: "Dan!" in a horrified tone.

Stiles went out into the hall. The butler was standing there, holding the door open. He handed Stiles' hat to him, bowed, and shut the door carefully after him when he went out.

RAIN SPATTERED THE hotel window in short, snappy bursts, coating the glass with a greasy film that slid slowly downward but never seemed to reach the bottom of the sash.

Stiles lay on the bed, smoking a cigarette. His eyes looked bitter and a little tired.

The telephone on the wall next to the door tinkled a few times and then finally rang.

Stiles put the receiver against his ear. "All right," he said. "Begin."

It was Raimler. His voice was worried and angry. "Stiles, what the hell are you playing at, anyway? Why don't you watch that half-witted brother-in-law of yours?"

Stiles said wearily: "What's he done now?"

"It's Bradford. I knew he'd cut loose. He owns a place called the *Tip-Top Club* on that little goose-neck of the city that runs out into Hagar's Swamp. Georgeson is out there now at what's supposed to be a whoop-it-up-before-election party.

"It's a frame. Bradford is sore. He knows if he tips over Georgeson's applecart the big boys of the machine will let him come back in again. He's put your sister wise and has the boys here all set to pull the joint as soon as she has time to get there and start things. Photographers from the papers here now, waiting to go on the raid. Oh, Bradford's got things fixed right! And I'm going to lead the raid—*me!* Everybody knows I'm not in with the organization, and they figure the reform crowd can't squawk about a frame if I start the stink. Get out there and stop this, Stiles. I can hold the raid off for a while."

Stiles said quickly: "All right, Raimler." His smile was wolfishly hard.

He hung up the receiver, put on his coat and picked up his hat. Then he stopped short, snapping his teeth with his thumbnail. He took off his coat again and put on a shoulder-holster he took out of a drawer in the dresser. He took his revolver from under the pillow on the bed and slipped it in the holster, adjusting the spring-clip carefully around the cylinder. Then he put his coat on again and went out the door.

STILES RENTED A coupé that had a nick out of the bottom of the windshield just in front of the steering-wheel. A thin dribble of rain blew through the nick and spattered on Stiles' leg. He cursed monotonously to himself and tried to move his leg out of the stream of water and still keep his foot on the accelerator.

Street-lights flipped by, one after the other, getting farther and farther apart. Finally they stopped and the pavement ended in a graveled road.

Stiles kept the car at top speed, skidding and bumping through the pools of muddy water. The road was twisting now between black, swishing walls that turned into green bushes when the headlights hit them.

Stiles tried to jerk another notch of speed out of the coupé and then caught a glimpse of a big sign with the red words *Tip-Top Club* and an arrow pointing.

He swung the coupé. The headlights splashed on a ditch full of dirty water, a white fence, some dripping brush, and finally a narrow, muddy road.

The coupé ground raggedly in low up to the long colonial porch. A few windows winked solemnly through the rain.

Stiles got out of the coupé and, leaning against the wind, stumbled up the steps and pounded on the door.

After a moment it opened, and a voice on the level with the first button of Stiles' coat said:

"Sorry, guy. We ain't servin' tonight."

Stiles said: "Get the hell out of the way." He pushed the door open and entered.

The big room was half-dark, tables shrouded in striped canvas covers. Behind a closed door on the other side of the dance-floor Stiles could hear Margaret's voice rising hysterically and Bradford being jolly and sympathetic.

"What room's Georgeson in?" Stiles asked.

The little bow-legged man in front of him stared up, his mouth open a little. "Hey! Who're you? What's the idea, huh?"

"There's a hitch, you fool!" Stiles said savagely. "What room's Georgeson in? That ain't his wife—it's his sister. I tried to head her off."

"Eighteen," the little man said. "But, listen, guy, Sol said—"

Stiles hit him. The little man went over a table, lit on a chair, and sprawled on the floor, kicking his short legs in the air.

Stiles was across the room, pounding up the broad stairs. He saw the door of the office open, caught a glimpse of the flat, pink circle that was Bradford's face, saw him open his mouth to shout something. Then Stiles was at the top of the stairs, running along the short hall.

He stopped before the door numbered 18, turned the knob. It was unlocked, and he burst in, slamming the door behind him.

He said: "Well, you damned fat-head, you!"

Georgeson was sitting on the couch under a reading lamp with his coat and vest off. His face was slick with perspiration, his hair mussed.

A woman with bright yellow hair sat beside him. She was dressed in a red dress cut low in front.

Stiles stared, contempt in his eyes, in the lines around his mouth, in his voice when he said:

"You need a nursemaid. Don't you know a frame when you see it? Margaret's downstairs."

Georgeson was getting up, his face twisted with anger. But at the last sentence he sat down again, opened his mouth and then shut it.

"Margaret!" he said, putting his hand over his mouth.

Stiles said bitterly: "Begins to sink in, does it? There isn't any before-election pep meeting here tonight. Bradford isn't one of your supporters. And this isn't his wife or his sister, or whatever he told you she was. You're framed, you fool! Bradford tipped Margaret off, and has the police ready to pull the joint. There'll be photographs in all the morning papers. What a fine chance you'll have to be mayor after this!"

Georgeson made helpless protesting noises, opening and shutting his mouth loosely.

Stiles laughed savagely. "Oh, yes, I'm a crook, and I was going to shake you down! You had everything figured out—figured out *wrong*. Sol Bradford—your faithful supporter! What a laugh!"

"No! Not Sol! He wouldn't—"

The woman laughed. "Yes, he would. And it's too late to do anything about it. Too late for even your smart friend, here."

The door of the room swung open while she was talking.

Stiles got the revolver out of his shoulder-holster, whirled around, dropped on one knee. Shots battered out from the doorway, hurried, confused. Two men firing close together.

Stiles shot back, emptying his revolver in a smashing blur of sound that drummed back and forth on the walls. One of the men in the doorway plunged straight forward as though he were diving at Stiles. He fell short, hit the floor with a crash. His hands, outspread in front of him, clenched and gathered the rug up into twin humps.

The other man dropped his gun and doubled over, hands on his stomach. He screamed in a hoarse voice and ran into the room, blindly, head down. He tripped over a chair and fell on the floor, still screaming.

The woman hadn't moved. She was looking down at the front of her dress. A dark stain was spreading over the bright red. She looked up suddenly.

"Why," she said in a surprised tone. "Why—" She started to laugh. She slid slowly lower on the couch. Then she stopped moving. Her eyes were wide open. The stain kept spreading across her dress.

Georgeson moaned a little, watching her. Stiles was reloading his revolver.

"They shot her," Georgeson said to him. "They shot her by mistake. They were aiming at you but they shot her." He shuddered suddenly.

Stiles caught up Georgeson's coat and hat, grabbed him by the arm and swung him towards the door. "Put these on and get out of here," he said in a strained voice.

They went down the hall. Georgeson, his eyes wide and unseeing went straight ahead, until, at the head of the stairs, a bullet knocked chips out of the wall beside him.

Stiles jerked him back. The little bow-legged man was a twisted blur at the bottom of the stairs. His gun smashed out again, flame slanting up. Stiles came down the stairs three at a time. Ten feet from the bottom he tripped and plunged head foremost.

The little man half-turned, tried to dodge. The full weight of Stiles' body hit him between the shoulders, and they both crashed on the floor.

Stiles got up slowly. The little man lay with his mouth open as though he were breathing heavily. Only he was not breathing.

Behind the lighted door of the private office Margaret was screaming. Stiles steadied himself against the wall and then walked wearily towards the door. He was almost there when Margaret ran out. Stiles kicked her feet from under her and she fell heavily.

Bradford was in the doorway. The pink in his face had faded and left his red lips standing out like ridges.

"Bradford," Stiles said dully. "Bradford."

They both shot at once. Bradford's bullet hit Stiles in the leg above the knee. He turned clear around and dropped on the floor, catching himself on his hands. With a great effort he turned back towards the door.

Bradford was standing there, looking at him, his mouth open a little. He tried to raise the gun in his hand, and it fell on the floor. He choked and coughed loosely, looking at the gun.

"Oh, hell," he said slowly and clearly. He started back in to his office. With his hand on the knob, he fell, opening the door as he did so. Half in the office his big body lay squashily flat on the floor.

Georgeson was coming down the stairs, his eyes still wide and dull.

"You beast!" Margaret screamed at him in a theatrical voice, raising her hands dramatically. "You beast! See what you've brought me to!"

Stiles got up. His leg would still hold his weight. Margaret's voice was like a rapidly receding echo in a long cave.

Stiles took his handkerchief from his pocket. He picked up Bradford's gun in the handkerchief and, walking over to the little man's body, aimed carefully and fired at him. Then he emptied the gun into the wall back of the staircase and threw it on the floor near Bradford. He wiped off his own gun and dropped it beside the little man.

Stiles stopped and looked at the floor. There was something wrong. A noise. Stiles tried to listen through the buzzing sound inside his head. Suddenly he knew. It was a siren. Coming fast.

"Shut up!" he said to Margaret. "Georgeson was framed. Just dumb, not crooked. Get out quick. Police 're coming."

He led the way through the kitchen, falling over things in the blackness. Margaret and Georgeson pressed close behind him. There was a rasp of brakes from the front and the sound of feet on the porch.

Stiles got the back door open, and they went out into wet darkness. They went wide around some shrubs that dripped and swished invisibly.

There were two police cars in the drive, but the front porch was empty except for Raimler. He stood hunched over, rain dripping slowly from his turned-down hat brim.

Margaret slipped and fell in the mud with a little splashing noise. Raimler looked in their direction and then turned and went back into the building.

"Bring your car?" Stiles asked Georgeson.

Georgeson shook his head mechanically. "Sol—Bradford brought me."

Stiles said: "Both of you get in Margaret's car. I'll push. Coast down the lane. Start the engine in road." He was beginning to have difficulty with his words.

"We—" Georgeson began, swallowing.

Stiles said: "Get the hell in that car."

"Thank—" Georgeson began again.

Stiles said: "Get in car, damn you!"

Georgeson and Margaret got in and Stiles heaved against the back of the heavy sedan. The mud was thick and Stiles' wounded leg kept slipping out from under him.

Raimler was suddenly beside him. "I'll help," he said and heaved against the car. It coasted silently down the lane. After it turned out on the road the engine bucked, choked, and then spluttered into an even sound that faded rapidly.

Raimler put his face close to Stiles' in the darkness. "You sure fixed things, didn't you?"

Stiles said: "Listen close. Little guy was up in room 18, seeing dame there. Two other guys bust in on them. They shoot dame. Little guy shoots them. Bradford hears. Tackles little guy as he comes downstairs. Shoot each other. Good enough?"

"You didn't leave very many witnesses. The big boys won't dare squawk. Yeah, I'll make it stick. But not with you here. Get in your car and get the hell out."

Stiles said: "Can't drive. Shot leg." Raimler said: "Oh, hell! Your car. What the hell will I do with that car? They'll trace you through it."

Stiles chuckled a little. "No. Rented it tonight. In Bradford's name."

"My God!" Raimler said slowly, at last. "You don't miss any bets. Go on down the road and wait for me. I'll pick you up in one of the squad cars. I'll have to beat it back inside now or some of those rummies will be out here nosing around."

Stiles went on down the lane. Raimler was running back towards the house. His voice sounded faintly, telling somebody to get to work and stop standing around like a fish-faced baboon.

Stiles tripped and fell down in the mud. He got up slowly, staggering. Walking very slowly and carefully he got to the road before he fell again. He lay there with his face against the wet gravel, and the rain pelted soddenly on his back.

An engine roared suddenly in the yard. Headlights swept in a flat circle. Stiles got up and stood swaying beside the road.

Raimler pulled the squad car to a stop, racing the engine.

"Get in, hurry up."

Stiles put his foot on the running-board and then fell straight over backwards into the ditch alongside the road. Raimler cursed in a high-pitched monotone, got out of the car, and splashed in the ditch beside him.

"Stiles! Stiles!" he said holding Stiles' head above the muddy water.

Stiles' head rolled loosely. "All right," he said. "All right. Help me up."

"My God!" Raimler said bitterly. "I'm sure going to earn that job! Why didn't you tell me you was hit bad? You trying to bleed to death on me just for spite?"

"Sorry," Stiles said dimly. "Sorry."

Raimler's voice was half-angry, half-worried. "Aw, shut up, damn you! Hold still while I heave you up in." He lifted Stiles, and staggered with his burden towards the car. "The new mayor'll owe something on this," he grunted, "but I can't cash it without you."

Kansas City Flash

Mark Hull investigates why a man looking for an autograph should get a bullet

THE PLACE SMELLED of ether. The hallway had a green-carpeted floor and smooth white walls. There were doors at regular intervals along the hall, and little red bulbs above the doors. Everything was quiet.

Pete Endor came out of one of the doors carrying a white porcelain dish with a towel over it. He shut the door carefully behind him and came noiselessly down the hall on crepe rubber soles. He was short and pale, with slicked-down black hair. He was dressed in a white duck uniform. He raised his eyebrows at Mark Hull and said:

"Be with you in a minute. Guy just shot his breakfast all over the floor."

He went on down the hall, around a turn. After a little he came back with a mop, made a sour face at Mark Hull, and went back in the room he had come out of.

Mark Hull sat down in the chair beside the glass-topped table that had more porcelain dishes and shiny steel instruments piled on top of it in orderly rows. He took a battered pack of cigarettes out of his vest pocket, selected one, and straightened it out between his thick, scarred fingers. He snapped a match on his thumbnail and blew some smoke at the white ceiling.

He was short and heavily muscled with broad, sloping shoulders and arms that were too long for the rest of him. His nose was plastered flat against his face. One cheek was criss-crossed with small white scars, and that side of his face looked slightly out of line. His eyes were small and blue and twinkling—set far apart. He appeared to be hard-boiled and good-humored at the same time. He looked like he was enjoying himself. He was a cynically tolerant spectator of the flea circus that is Hollywood.

He whistled through his teeth softly, tapping his foot on the floor. Pete Endor came out of the room again, holding the mop carefully away from him. He went down the hall. He came back without the mop.

"If this isn't a hell of a job," he said.

"That what you called me over to tell me?" Mark Hull asked, letting smoke dribble out of his flattened nostrils.

"You heard anything about Doro Faliv?"

"Hell, yes," said Mark Hull. "So's everybody else that can read. What she eats, and what she thinks, and what she wears. And how it feels to get five thousand dollars a week and be a motion picture star. And what she does to get sex appeal. What do you want, an introduction?"

Pete's eyes got big. "Do you know her?"

Mark Hull snorted smoke. "Only when I see her. Listen, dope, you can't sign any contracts, so she wouldn't be interested in you. Now if it's not too much trouble, just tell me what you wanted and leave the fan mail for some other time."

Pete leaned over. He looked both ways cautiously. He put his sleek head to one side and listened elaborately. He'd seen a gangster picture the night before and knew how it was done. Mark Hull waited with a pained but patient expression.

"I got a hot tip," said Pete mysteriously.

"Look out it don't burn your fingers."

"Do I get a cut?" asked Pete.

"You get a smack on the snozzle in about a minute."

"Listen," said Pete, talking out of the corner of his mouth. "Night before last they brought a little dope in here with a couple of bullets in him. He'd been shot, see?"

"Oh," Mark Hull said sarcastically. "You mean he'd been shot."

Pete nodded seriously. "Shot. Nothing the docs could do. He passed out this morning. I was there." He winked. "I was right there."

"What about it?"

"He was an autograph hound," Pete said. "He came to just before he died, and he told me all about it. Before the doc got there. He collected autographs. Autographs of all the stars. He had them in a little book. He had five hundred of 'em." Pete stopped and chewed a fingernail. "I only got three hundred."

"I suppose he tried to collect Doro Faliv's autograph, and she got sore and put a couple of bullets in him."

Pete nodded triumphantly. "That's it!"

Mark Hull choked on cigarette smoke. He coughed hackingly. When it was over he stared at Pete with amazed eyes.

"You mean that's actually what he said?"

Pete nodded again. "Yup. Only the guy that was with her did the shooting."

"My ——!" said Mark Hull quietly. "My ——!" He pulled up his coat sleeve and pinched himself on his hairy forearm. He took off his hat and wiped his brow. He fanned himself with his hat. Suddenly he glared at Pete with narrowed eyes.

"You mugg, are you makin' this up?"

Pete shook his head and held up his right hand. "It's the honest truth, Mr. Hull."

Mark Hull blinked his eyes and gave a long whistle. "Tell me just what he said."

"Well, he lives—lived—in an apartment house near Tenth and Western. *The Forsage Arms.* That night about eleven he was comin' out of the building to go down to a drug-store and get some smokes. Just as he was comin' down the steps a car stopped at the curb. Doro Faliv got out."

"Wait a minute," said Mark Hull. "How'd he know it was her? They look different off the screen."

"He used to hang around the *Brown Derby* all the time gettin' autographs, and he'd seen her lots of times, but there was always such a crowd around her that he couldn't get her autograph. It's terrible how that crowd pushes you around, Mr. Hull. What I mean, it really is. Why, one time I—"

"Go on, go on," said Mark Hull through clenched teeth.

"What happened after he saw her?"

"He thought this was a good chance to get her autograph. He always carried his book with him. You can't never tell when you're gonna meet a star. Why, one time I saw John Barrymore—"

Mark Hull made a strangling noise.

Pete came back to the subject hurriedly. "So he walks up to her, and he says: 'Hello, Miss Faliv. Will you sign my autograph book?' And then *blooie!* He didn't remember nothing else until he came to here just before he died. They found him up in Hollywoodland lying in some brush along the road."

"Anyone else know this?"

"No. I think it's terrible, Mr. Hull, when they shoot you for just asking for an autograph. They get awful sore sometimes, though. I remember once when I—"

Mark Hull stood up and rammed a blunt forefinger into Pete Endor's chest.

"You keep your mouth shut about this. If it's a straight tip you get a couple hundred. If it's a phoney I'll come back here and spatter your brains all over the wall."

MARK HULL SQUEEZED his bulk into a telephone booth in a drug-store on Sunset Boulevard, a block from the hospital. He pushed a nickel in the slot and dialed a number.

"Dolan, Scenario Department," he said when a feminine voice answered.

He waited, tapping on the top of the telephone with his fingernail and whistling softly. His eyes were gleaming. He looked like he was getting a big kick out of things in general.

"Yeah?" It was a thin, flat, very weary voice.

"Listen, Dolan, this is Mark Hull. I want to see a guy on the lot that don't want to see me. Can I use your name to get in?"

There was an audible sigh. "Yeah," said the voice tonelessly. The line went dead.

Mark Hull came out of the drugstore, got in his battered Ford coupé and drove down Sunset. He turned off on a side street, parked the Ford at the curb. He walked along a high cement wall with big signs advertising motion pictures along the top of it. He walked past an iron gate with a khaki uniformed policeman sitting on a stool beside it. He went in a glass door with an iron grilling on it.

It was a small room with a green tile floor and walls. There was a long bench along one wall, a potted plant in one corner, and a big desk in another. A closed door with three steps leading up to it was in the middle of the back wall.

The blond youth behind the desk smiled and said "Yes?" courteously.

"I want to see Mr. Dolan," Mark Hull said. "Hull's the name. He's expecting me."

The blond youth repeated: "Mr. Dolan." He picked up a telephone that was the only furnishing on the desk and said: "Mr. Dolan," into it. He waited patiently.

After a little he said: "There's a Mr. Hull to see you."

He listened. He hung up the receiver, tore a blank off a yellow pad of paper, scribbled on it.

"Through that door," he said. "You know where to go?"

Mark Hull nodded, took the slip, went up the three steps. He went through the door, closed it behind him. He was in a short, dark corridor with doors with frosted glass panes on either side. He walked down the corridor and out another door into the sunlight. He followed a cement walk through a small lawn and was in a narrow street flanked on each side by two-story, barn-like buildings with corrugated iron doors.

There were some cowboys sitting around in the shade, smoking and talking in low tones. They looked hot and tired. A soldier went by dragging his rifle behind him, his hob-nails clanking on the cement. Two girls in evening dresses followed him. In a doorway three men in horn-rimmed glasses and golf knickers were arguing earnestly. A supervisor went by, walking alone and talking to himself.

Mark Hull turned a corner and was in front of a Spanish-style building with white walls and a red tile roof. He went up the stairs, along a hall, and entered a door. A girl with honey-colored hair and very red lips sat at a big desk against one wall.

Mark Hull rested his big hands on the desk and leaned forward.

"Mr. Schrimer in?"

She was shaking her head wearily before he had even started to say anything.

"No. Have you an appointment?"

Mark Hull took one of his cards from his pocket, picked up the pencil on the desk and wrote: "Doro Faliv," on the card.

"Take this to him," he said. "Right now."

The girl looked at the card. She turned it over and read what he had written on the back. Her blue eyes got very big and round.

She said: "Sit down a moment, please," in a choked, hurried voice. She got up and went through a door with polished mahogany panels.

Mark Hull made a triumphant clicking noise with his tongue. He snapped his fingers, grinning, and winked in a blowing way at the wall opposite him.

"I got something this time!" he whispered to himself. "Hot damn!"

The girl came back.

"Mr. Schrimer will see you. Come this way, please."

Mark Hull followed her, walking with a confident, springy sway—big shoulders back, thick chest pushed out.

Schrimer's office looked almost as gaudy as the motion picture sets of motion picture magnates' offices. It was big and impressive with soft carpets and paneled walls and pensive pictures and period furniture.

Schrimer was behind the desk under a big window at the side of the room. He was small and white and pink-eyed. He looked like a scared rabbit peering over a log. He made a vague stuttering noise and waved to a chair in front of the desk.

Mark Hull waited until the girl had gone, closing the door behind her. He rocked back and forth on, his heels, staring at Schrimer with one thick eyebrow cocked up quizzically. After a moment he stepped softly to the door and suddenly opened it.

A fat man was standing there, bent over, with his eyes on the level with the keyhole. His round, mournful face didn't change expression in the slightest. He straightened up and sighed sadly. Coming inside the office, he closed the door behind him and leaned against the wall with his hands in his pockets, staring glumly at Mark Hull.

Mark Hull smiled pleasantly at him and said: "Hello, McNulty. It's a wonder to me you don't get cross-eyed with all the keyhole peeping you do." He sat down in the chair in front of the desk and took out a cigarette. "Have one?" he said politely, offering the pack to Schrimer.

"Y-you know him?" Schrimer asked McNulty.

McNulty nodded gloomily. "Yeah. Name of Mark Hull. Used to be a stunt-man. Got that mugg when he jumped off a three-story building and the net busted. Picks up money now running around and doing hush-hush jobs for the studios. Tough egg."

Mark Hull bowed and smiled. "Glad to meet you, Mr. Schrimer."

Schrimer looked like a rabbit all ready to get impudent with a lion that was safely caged up.

"W-what do you know about Doro Faliv?" he asked importantly.

Mark Hull rumpled his bristly hair, frowning. "I know she's five feet three, has black hair and come-hither eyes and—"

"Cut the clowning," said McNulty.

"How much is it costing you a day?" Mark Hull asked, suddenly serious.

Schrimer waved his skinny arms. "T-ten thousand d-dollars a d-day! That's what it's costing me! T-ten thousand d-dollars every d-day! I got p-p-production schedules to meet—"

"How long has she been gone?"

"T-two days."

"How much do they want?"

"F-fifty thousand d-dollars! F-fifty thousand d-dollars! In these hard t-times—" He stopped and blinked his pink eyes at Mark Hull. "How d-did you know?"

Mark Hull leaned back in his chair and folded his arms. He smiled complacently. "I get around. I get around."

McNulty made a disgusted noise in his throat. "Listen, mugg, we haven't got time to play guessing games with you. What's the big idea?"

Mark Hull shrugged. "Maybe I could sell a story to the newspapers."

McNulty shook his head seriously. "Nix, brother. This isn't funny business. One slip, and Faliv gets it." He drew his forefinger across his throat and made a clicking noise. "She's worth a couple million dollars to this studio. We can't afford to have you running around squawking. We got lots of nice dark places to shut mouthy guys in. Get it off your chest before you get tapped on the conk and slung in one of them."

Mark Hull said: "How much for getting her back all in one piece and without any noise?"

Schrimer looked at McNulty inquiringly. McNulty nodded.

"F-five thousand d-dollars cash."

Mark Hull stood up. "Okey. Make a memorandum of that and sign it."

"Now listen," McNulty said, "you got a tip on where she is. It must be a hot one because this business is strictly under cover. We can't have you stumbling around putting your feet in things. How much will you take to go home and play solitaire and let us work your tip?"

Mark Hull shook his head. "Ixnay. I like trouble. And don't let me catch any of your bloodhounds trailing around, either."

THERE WERE POTTED plants around the tiled lobby of *The Forsage Arms* and a red and black rubber rug on the floor. Over in one corner was a small desk with a switchboard at the end. A tall, bald man with a toothy grin was behind the desk.

He looked over the top of his glasses at Mark Hull and made pleasant little clucking noises.

Mark Hull leaned over the desk and winked at him "Married?" he asked in a whisper.

The clerk looked wall-eyed. His lips pursed up. He nodded blankly.

Mark Hull poked him in the chest with his thumb and grinned with one side of his mouth. "I'm lookin' for a guy's wife for him."

The clerk ceased to look blank. His eyes glistened. He licked his thin lips and nodded eagerly. He had the sly look of a villain in a movie serial.

Mark Hull held up a twenty-dollar bill. "She's about five-three. Slim. Swell legs. Black hair. She'd be wearing a real heavy veil. She'd be with two or maybe three guys. Hard-looking boys. Whenever she came down here one of the guys would have a good hold on her, like he was afraid she'd run away."

The clerk nodded eagerly. "Yeah. She was here. Two guys. She went out this morning with one guy. He paid his bill. Said he was moving. The other guy is up in the apartment now. Packing up, I guess. They were in a hurry."

"What apartment?"

"18-E. It's on the fifth floor."

"If he comes down while I'm going up, hold him here with some stall until I get back," Mark Hull ordered, relinquishing the twenty and exhibiting another one.

The clerk nodded again. He watched Mark Hull stalk across the lobby and enter the elevator. "These women," he said.

MARK HULL GOT out of the elevator and waited until

the boy had sent it downward. He slid along the thickly carpeted hall, looking at door numbers. He found 18-E at the end of the corridor.

He knocked softly. His lips were drawn into a tight, lop-sided grin. He blew on the knuckles of his right fist and held it poised hip-high, balancing on his toes. His eyes were wide and excited looking.

Somebody moved softly in the apartment. Mark Hull knocked again.

"Janitor," he said in a thick voice.

The door opened, and a round, greasy-looking face appeared. "What—"

Mark Hull's knuckles connected with the face with a sound like a bursting balloon. The door jerked open. There was a gurgling noise, and the sound of a heavy fall. Mark Hull went through the door and closed it behind him.

The greasy-faced one was getting up off the floor, spitting curses. The rest of him matched his face. He was small and stoop-shouldered and bandy-legged. His hair curled in oiled ringlets. His mouth was thick-lipped, blubbery.

He found a knife somewhere and dived for Mark Hull, slashing upward. Mark Hull stepped sidewise, caught the knife hand, and twisted it until the knife clattered on the floor, blocking kicks at his abdomen with one knee. He slammed short, choppy rights into the center of the greasy face.

The other one flopped backward over a chair, crashed full length on the floor. Mark Hull got a handful of coat front, hauled him up.

"Where'd you take her?" he asked very softly holding a big fist in front of the greasy face.

The thick lips said: "Police b——!" and writhed wetly.

Mark Hull let the fist go. The other went head-first over the couch into the corner behind it. His short, crooked legs stayed in sight for an instant, then slid limply downward.

Mark Hull dragged him from under the couch plopped him down on the cushions. He sat there stared vacantly ahead with his big mouth twitching loosely. Mark Hull scraped a chair over and sat down facing the couch. He took a .38 Colt automatic from his shoulder-holster.

Consciousness suddenly flicked back into the greasy one's eyes.

"Police b——!" he said.

Mark Hull swiped him with the automatic. He flopped over on the couch. Mark Hull pulled him upright. He said levelly:

"I'm not from the police. I'm from the studio. We're going to play this game until you tell me where your new hide-out is."

"Go to hell!"

Mark Hull cracked him again.

"I'm not fooling. You can blow after you tell me. You mugg, don't you know a studio will never pay on a rig like this?"

Saliva made wet threads down from the blubbery lips. He sniffled, covering his face with his hands, peering at Mark Hull through stained fingers.

"Pasadena," he said thickly.

Mark Hull raised the gun. The greasy one rolled away on the couch, whining.

"No, no! Santa Monica. First and Tracy. An old white apartment house."

Mark Hull hit him carefully, calculatingly. This time on top of the head. He went down with a long, whistling sigh. Mark

Hull left him there, nosed around in the apartment. He found two half-packed suit-cases on the bed, a small trunk on the floor. He came back in the front room carrying several bath towels that were wringing wet.

He tied the greasy one carefully with the towels and a hand-kerchief in the slack mouth.

"There, baby," he said cheerfully. "If you get out of that daddy'll give you a big red lolly-pop."

Mark Hull straightened his tie, smoothed down his bristly hair. He put his hat on carefully, tipping it down over one eye. He went to the door and opened it.

A bent little old lady with her hand cupped behind one jar nearly fell into the apartment. She straightened up quickly, making flustered sounds.

"I heard a noise. A sort of horrible bumping noise."

Mark Hull closed the door carefully behind him, making sure the lock clicked.

"Bosco," he said.

"Bosco?" the old lady repeated blankly.

Mark Hull nodded easily. "Yeah. Bosco, the Dog-Faced Boy. He's in the movies. I'm his manager. He's only half-human. He got excited a minute ago and tried to brain me with a hammer. I had quite a time with him before I could get him back in his strait-jacket. I think he got hold of some raw meat."

The old lady's eyes were like glass marbles. "Half-human," she repeated in a horrified voice. "Raw meat! Strait-jacket!" Her mouth snapped shut. She hobbled up the hall, whisked in a door. The door slammed emphatically. The key grated in the lock.

Mark Hull grinned widely. He tipped his hat further over

his eye. He puffed out his big chest and strutted down the hall towards the elevator. He looked well pleased with himself.

THE APARTMENT HOUSE was a two-story, square building. It had been stuccoed, and the stucco was peeling off at the corners, showing bare brown boards underneath. Sickly looking vines on a shaky trellis curled over the front and did their best to hide the ravages of time. The lawn and the hedge needed trimming, and the two big plants on either side of the front door looked shabbily discouraged.

Mark Hull pressed his broad thumb against the button that was underneath a white card with "Manager" written on it. A small, thin woman opened the door instantly. She had stringy brown hair and mouse-like brown eyes. She watched Mark Hull timidly.

Mark Hull took off his hat and smiled. He looked genial and good-natured in a hard-boiled way. He chuckled at her.

"They get all settled?" he asked.

The landlady's lips formed the word: "Who?" noiselessly.

Mark Hull took out his wallet and found a twenty-dollar bill. The landlady's eyes got very large and wistful.

Mark Hull said: "I'm a friend of theirs. I'm sorry for them. They've had it plenty tough. Did they pay you anything in advance?"

She shook her head without taking her eyes from the twenty.

"Did they move in this morning?" he asked. "Just the two of them. The lady veiled."

She nodded.

"What room?"

"Ten. In back. On the first floor." She spoke in a barely audible monotone.

"Take this as a down payment on the rent," Mark Hull said.

The bill disappeared out of his fingers down the front of the landlady's dress in a split-second. She was gone as instantly as she had appeared. Mark Hull blinked in a surprised way.

He went silently down the gloomy hall that was thick with the smell of unventilated rooms. He found a door that had a 1 and an 0 pinned on it haphazardly. He frowned at the door. His hand started to move towards his shoulder-holster. He shook his head and took the hand away again.

"All in one piece," he whispered to himself, "and without any noise." He made a worried face at the door. The man inside was a killer. Then he shrugged. Have to take the chance.

He knocked lightly on the door. "Hey," he said, "I'm sorry to bodder yuh but de old lady says I gotta put some new light bulbs in because dem you got is all boined out."

There was a pause. Mark Hull held his breath. Then the door opened a little, and a hand appeared. A voice said:

"Give 'em to me."

Mark Hull got hold of the wrist and slammed his shoulder against the door. There was a bump and a strangled grunt. Mark Hull got inside and kicked the door shut behind him.

A thin dark-faced man twisted his wrist free with one graceful motion. In a continuation of the same motion he slammed three quick blows into Mark Hull's face. He danced away easily and lightly. He had dark, wavy hair and a thin, viciously handsome face. He was in a white shirt and dark trousers. He grinned at Mark Hull, showing white teeth through thin, red lips.

Mark Hull grunted and shook his head. There were red marks on his scarred face. He jerked off his hat and tossed it on the floor behind him. He came forward, slouched a little, thick arms swinging at his sides.

The thin man danced in again, moving with a peculiar effortless weave. His fists found Mark Hull's face, and then he was ten feet away, grinning. He was faster than greased lightning.

"Well?" he said. "Well?"

Mark Hull breathed noisily through his flattened nose. He shuffled forward, swaying a little. His eyes were coldly glinting slits. He tried to catch the thin man's arms as he came in. The thin man was too fast. A ring on his finger cut Mark Hull over one eye.

The thin man danced on his toes, weaving his shoulders loosely. Evidently he could see backward. He dodged around chairs and tables without looking behind him. He was grinning still. He was having a fine time.

"Well?" he said. "Want to quit and talk it over?"

Mark Hull kept shuffling forward. His lips were flat against his teeth in a soundless snarl. The thin man circled backward effortlessly. He was as graceful as a snake. He could move six feet to Mark Hull's one.

"Dance, damn you!" Mark Hull said thickly. "Wait till I get hold of you."

"You won't," said the thin man. "You can't touch me."

He battered Mark Hull's groping hands aside disdain, fully, put three cracking blows into his face, and was leaning against the wall on the other side of the room all in the same second.

"All right," he said, sliding easily along the wall and watching Mark Hull follow him stubbornly. "Private flattie from the studio, aren't you, boy? You don't want a stink any worse than I do. We'll wake the whole damned place if we keep at it. I'm willing to talk business. Let's be nice."

Mark Hull shrugged and straightened up. His eyes were glittering dangerously. He wasn't used to being beaten.

"Okey," he said. "What's your proposition?"

The thin man relaxed, still grinning. Mark Hull suddenly dived at him head-first. The thin man wasn't there. Mark Hull crashed head-on into the wall. He fell heavily on his face on the floor. He rolled dizzily, and the thin man dropped on him, knees first.

Mark Hull tried to twist out of it, but the thin man's fingers were digging into his throat. Mark Hull hit upward blindly. The thin man rolled his head expertly with the blows. His fingers kept digging in.

Mark Hull arched his body up on his heels and tried to get at his shoulder-holster, but the thin man blocked that with his leg. Mark Hull's tongue was big and thick in his mouth, and there was a purple haze shot with exploding orange spots in front of his eyes.

"You asked for it," the thin man said gleefully.

His voice was a squeaky whisper through the roaring in Mark Hull's ears. His dark face receded dimly through the purple haze. There were iron bands around Mark Hull's chest. He choked and writhed, suddenly frantic.

The thin man's fingers loosened. His viciously handsome face was blank, incredulous. He let go of Mark Hull's throat and got slowly and heavily to his feet. His arms were hanging limply. He turned around, and Mark Hull saw the butcher knife that was up to the hilt in his back.

The thin man took a step forward. His voice came thickly—"You—" he said. "You—"

Doro Faliv stood ten feet away. Her slim body was erectly

rigid. Her dark eyes were enormously wide. She made small, terrorized sounds in her throat—like a frightened child.

Mark Hull came out of his daze in time to hook his foot around the thin man's ankle. The thin man made no effort to catch himself, to ease his fall. He slammed down limply all at once. He moved a little on the rug. His hands went out in front of him, clutching. His feet jerked in short little kicks. He made soft, choking noises. Then he stopped moving suddenly, as though he were a mechanical toy that had run down.

Mark Hull got stiffly to hands and knees and crawled to him. He turned the thin man over. He grunted and let the thin man fall back again. He looked up at Doro Faliv.

SHE WAS STILL standing rigid. Tears washed wet little paths down her cheeks. She sniffled. She looked like a crying schoolgirl.

She was one of the real mysteries of Hollywood. She was thin and flat-chested, with a complexion like yellow paste. Her black hair was lifeless and dull. Her features were assembled in regular enough order, but her face gave a queer blank effect, as though there was nothing but emptiness behind it. But on the screen she was marvelous.

She was the essence of allure. She could send goose-pimples along your back by just turning her head. The camera brought something out that wasn't there.

Mark Hull started to say something. He choked. He massaged his throat and tried it again.

"What happened?" he said wheezily.

"I went out to walk at night—alone." Her voice was full-throated and soft, but it, too, was lifeless. "They made me go

with them. They said if I didn't they'd throw acid in my face."
She looked at him slyly, like a little girl lying to her mother.

Mark Hull got slowly off the floor. He stood looking at her.
One side of his wide mouth lifted a little, showing his teeth.
Then he shrugged.

"You've got to get out of here. Quick."

He went scouting around, nosing in corners, under the bed, in
the bathroom. He looked for quite a while at an expensive black
bag he found in a closet. He found a hat and coat in the same
closet and helped her put them on. He pulled the veil over her face.

She accepted all this calmly, as a matter of course.

Mark Hull took hold of both her thin shoulders. He put his
tense, scarred face close to her blank one.

"Listen," he said, shaking her. "You're not to say a word about
this to anyone. Understand me?"

She nodded, looking a little puzzled.

Mark Hull took a key-ring from his pocket, separated one
key from the rest, and closed her hand around it. "This is the
key to the ignition on my Ford. It's parked down the street
that way—" he pointed "—a block. A yellow coupé. You get in
it and drive straight home and stay there."

She smiled shyly at him. "I can drive a Ford," she said.

Mark Hull grunted as though someone had hit him in the
stomach. He grabbed her by the shoulder and pushed her
towards the window. He helped her through, caught her under
the arms, and lowered her until her feet were on the ground.

"Now beat it!" he said explosively.

She looked up at him in a hurt, frightened way. He made a
savage gesture, and she stumbled hurriedly along the hedge
towards the front of the house.

He pulled his head back inside and shut the window. He made a wry face, shaking his head. Then he went out into the hall, locking the door behind him, and found the telephone on the table near the front door.

He looked around. Then he sat down and dialed long distance. He gave the number of the studio and waited, tapping on the table with his fingernails. His face was beginning to swell in lumpy bumps. The blood from the cut above his eye had trickled down his cheek and dried. The marks on his throat were changing from red to blue. He looked disgusted.

"Hello," he said after a while. "Give me McNulty.... Yeah, McNulty. That fat mugg that pretends to be a detective and goes around peeking through keyholes.... Well, find him.... All right." He waited impatiently.

It was some time before McNulty's mournful voice answered.

"McNulty speaking."

"This is Hull. Do you know a dark, thin guy with wavy hair and a nasty grin?"

"Sure," said McNulty. "That's the Kansas City Flash. He's bad. Indicted for murder three times. Beat all three raps. Served once for peddling dope—once for white slavery. Used to be a prizefighter."

"I know that now," Mark Hull said bitterly. "He just got through pasting hell out of me and was doing a nice job of choking me to death when your cute little star stuck a butcher knife in his back."

McNulty was quiet for quite a while. Then he said:

"Where is she now?"

"On her way home in my car. She gave me a sappy song-and-dance about being snatched by this Flash guy. Only she forgot that people that get kidnaped don't pack a bag take along with them."

"Uh-huh," McNulty said sadly. "She would forget that."

Mark Hull went on, talking in a low, vicious voice: "I collect my *ten* grand. She's in the clear. But the whole thing makes me sick at my stomach. By ——! I never dirtied my hands like this before. The Flash knocked off a guy that recognized her. The poor little devil asked her for an autograph. It was so awful damned useless."

"Uh-huh," said McNulty. "What do you think about it?"

"Me?" asked Mark Hull savagely. "Oh, I'm just in from the sticks. I think they were going up to his apartment to have a pleasant little chat about the political situation. I think they were just playing a cute joke when they shot that little punk and tried to shake the studio down for fifty thousand on a phoney kidnaping gag. It was just good clean fun when she saw the game was up and stuck a butcher knife in her boy-friend's back."

"Yeah," McNulty said slowly. "You been around Hollywood a long time. You know lots of things that aren't on the front pages. But I'll tell you something you don't know. This Kansas City Flash was her husband."

Mark Hull made a noise like a punctured tire. He goggled blankly at the wall.

McNulty went on: "You can imagine how we felt when we found it out. A half-million in advertising all shot to hell if anybody found out she had a heel with a record like his for a husband. Of course all this stuff about her being an exiled princess from some Asiatic country is just so much crap. One of the directors spotted her in a newsreel of a marathon dance.

Before that she was in a taxi dance-hall. I don't know what she was before that, but after one look at the Flash's record, I can make a pretty good guess."

Mark Hull said: "Is this straight?"

"Uh-huh. And that ain't all. He'd ditched her when she was sick about three years ago. She hadn't heard a word from him. But she was glad to see him when he turned up. He figured he was going to glom on to all her salary. But we had that fixed. She's got two contracts. One gives her fifty dollars a week. The other gives three thousand a week to a trust fund in her name controlled by a trustee appointed by the studio."

"I knew about that double contract," Mark Hull said slowly.

"Yeah. So did the Flash. That's why he tried his shakedown. We tried to tell her what he was. But it was no sale. He was her husband and he had told her he was framed, and so he was framed."

"She must be coo-coo."

"Uh-huh. Not coo-coo. Just dumb. She's got the mind of about a ten-year-old kid. You know how she looks and talks. I don't know why she is the way she is on the screen. Nobody can figure it out. She just is. All the directors are nuts to get a chance at doing one of her pictures. She'll do anything you tell her. She's got no ideas of her own. But, damn it, you can't help but like her. She tries so damned hard to please you."

Mark Hull nodded slowly. He was beginning to understand the way she had acted. That remark about knowing how to drive a Ford. A ten-year-old.

"I wonder why she stabbed him," he said, puzzled.

"She was nuts about her fans. She'd give them anything they asked for. When Flash shot the little autograph hound, it was curtains for him. She just waited for a good chance. Probably don't even realize it's murder."

"What'll we do with him?"

"I think maybe he was killed when he got drunk and fell in front of the Limited tonight somewhere out in the desert," McNulty said thoughtfully.

Mark Hull chuckled. He looked good-humored again in spite of his banged-up face. He told McNulty the address, and added: "You're not so dumb as you look, McNulty. I think if you had a real good friend that was a brain specialist, and he went down and looked in Apartment 18-E of *The Forsage Arms* he'd find a case there that should be shut in a nice, quiet place for a while, where he could cut out paper dolls without being bothered, and where people won't hear him talking to himself."

"You're not so dumb, either," said McNulty.

Hit and Run

And who wouldn't run when the other
guy is using brass knuckles

CLOUDS LIKE ROLLING smoky streamers chased each other across the dull sky, and rain whipped down in short, snappy bursts. Tait came hiking up Fifth, leaning against the wind, with the collar of his trench coat strapped tight around his thick throat, the brim of his soaked hat flapping against his nose. He shouldered through the crowd that was huddled close in the lee of the building on the corner of Hill, waiting for the signal bell to clang.

"Paiper! Paiper, Mr. Tait?"

Tait pulled the skirt of his trench coat aside, dug in his pocket. "Yeah, Ike. What's new?"

Ike shot a quick glance over his shoulder, then looked back at the private detective. "They let them dirty, murderin' rats off! Them three as robbed the bank out at Junction Bend six months back and murdered that poor young lad as was the teller there! Shot him down in cold blood, they did! And they got off scot-free!"

"That's the way it goes," Tait said philosophically.

The signal changed with a dull clang. The crowd jostled forward, carrying Tait along, an uncomfortable mass of umbrellas, slickers, rain coats, wet humanity. Across the street, Tait shook himself loose again, walked half-way down the block, turned into the lobby of a building. He nodded at the starter, ducked into an open elevator.

He got out at the eleventh floor, stood still at a bend in the corridor while he dug a pencil out of his pocket and marked a horse he wanted to bet on in the sixth race. He put the pencil away and walked down the corridor, still reading the paper. Automatically he stopped before a door that had "J.J. Tait. Private Investigator" printed in gold in neat block letters down in one corner, fumbled for the keys in his trousers pocket.

A voice behind him said: "Mr. Tait?"

Tait turned around. "Yes?"

She was nice. Very nice. She had on a brown coat, streaked with moisture, that looked stylish in spite of it. Brown over-shoes that came up halfway on very neat calves. A small brown hat with a down-turned brim that was slanted at a rakish angle. Blond hair damply curling, soft red lips, and eyes that were as blue as the clear sky on a summer day.

"May I—see you for a moment?" she asked timidly.

"Sure," said Tait. "Come on in." He pushed the door of the office open, followed her in. "Sit down."

He took off his soaked hat and trench coat, hung them on the rack in the corner. He was short and very thick through the chest, with broad sloping shoulders that rolled a little when he walked. There was a dent in the bridge of his nose, a short scar on one cheek. His eyes, small and blue and set wide apart, had a recklessly humorous glint to them. He looked as if he knew his way around.

He came over and sat down behind the desk. "Now what can I do for you?" he asked, fishing a battered pack of cigarettes out of his coat pocket and offering them to her.

She shook her head. She was sitting very straight in the chair, with her small gloved hands folded tightly on her lap. She was rigidly tense. She took a deep breath and swallowed, as though she were going to take a sudden plunge into cold water.

"Mr. Tait, my name is Glendon—Alice Glendon."

"Pleasure to know you," Tait said, snapping a match on his thumbnail.

She edged forward a little. "Mr. Tait, do I look like a criminal?"

Tait studied her critically through the match flame. "No," he said. "No, I wouldn't say that." He blew out a long plume of smoke.

"Well, I am!"

"Is that so?" Tait asked, politely interested.

She nodded soberly. "I was driving home about six o'clock last night. It was raining, you know." She stopped talking, and two big tears slid slowly down her cheeks.

Tait wiggled uncomfortably. "Now, now," he said clumsily. "It isn't as important as that."

"It is important! I was driving along the street, and it was dark, and there were a lot of lights glaring at me, and all of a sudden this man stepped out from between two parked cars not ten feet in front of me." She stopped and shuddered spasmodically.

"And then what?" Tait asked.

"I h-hit him! It was terrible! I tried to stop, and I couldn't, and the fender hit him with the awfulest sound, and he fell down on the pavement and rolled. Oh!" She put her hands up in front of her face. "I'll never forget it! Never!"

"What's criminal about that?" Tait asked. "It was his fault."

She nodded mutely. "But then—then—I didn't stop. I drove off."

"Oh," said Tait, rubbing his jaw with his thumb thoughtfully. "That makes it a little different. They get your number?"

She shook her head. "That isn't it! Don't you see? I hit that poor man and hurt him and then went away without stopping. I don't know what ever made me do it. But I was just panicky, and—and I did it!"

"Sure," Tait said. "I know how it is. It happens before you can think. But what do you want me to do?"

"I want you to find out how badly he was hurt and make some sort of a settlement with him."

"Sure," Tait repeated. "That's easy. Where'd the accident happen?"

"At Fourteenth and High."

Tait nodded. "Okey. And what's your address?"

"Apartment 322, *Fenwood Arms*, at Elm and Twenty-second."

Tait wrote it down. "All right, Miss Glendon. I'll fix everything up. First I'd better go to the hospital and look up this bird and see how badly he's hurt and have a talk with him. Then I'll let you know the dope, and we can figure out a settlement."

She stood up. "Thank you, Mr. Tait. I feel so much better already—as though you had taken a big load off my shoulders." She smiled up at him demurely. She could smile very nicely. "You're so strong and so confident of yourself that it gives me confidence, too." She held out her hand.

Tait took it gingerly. "Ah—yes," he said, clearing his throat. "I'll let you know later how things turn out."

He stood in the doorway of the office and watched her walk down the hall towards the elevators. She was just as nice to look at going away as she was coming forward.

Tait went back in the office and closed the door. He sat down behind the desk, tilted back in his chair and frowned at the ceiling. Alice Glendon was very dazzling to look at from close range. She had a very plausible story to tell, and she told it well. She shuddered at the right time, her voice quavered when it should have, and her tears came when they were needed. But somehow Tait wasn't convinced. Somehow he didn't believe that Alice Glendon was either as dumb or as helpless as she would have liked to have him believe. Although he couldn't put his finger on it, there was a distinctly phoney note somewhere.

Tait squinted at the ceiling and tugged at the lobe of one ear and said: "Hmm," to himself very thoughtfully.

A LITTLE LATER, Tait went up broad stone steps, pushed through swinging glass doors, and went into a large bare room with glistening white walls and ceiling and black rubber mats on the tiled floor. The smell of ether and disinfectant pinched his nostrils a little, and his heels thudded hard in the hushed silence as he went across to the small desk in one corner.

A nurse with a long nose and a long sour face looked up at him through thick spectacles and said: "Yes?" in a whisper.

"Do you have a record of ambulance calls?" Tait asked.

She nodded silently.

"Look up and tell me who was the interne that went out on the call to Fourteenth and High last night about six."

"Fourteenth and High," she repeated in her whisper. She thumbed through some records, looked up suddenly. "Fourteenth and High?"

Tait nodded. "Yes."

The nurse's face got a little longer and even more sour. She squinted at him over the tops of the thick glasses in a wordlessly suspicious way.

"Take your time," Tait said politely. "I'm in no hurry."

The nurse flushed, swallowing hard. "Mr. Sheedley was the *orderly* on the ambulance," she said stiffly. "The call came at a time when no doctor was available. He's on duty now. That way."

Tait followed her pointing finger, went back through the lobby, along a short corridor with gleaming white walls. The smell of ether was stronger now, and Tait snorted distastefully. He stopped before an open door.

There were two men playing checkers at a table in the corner. One wore the uniform of a chauffeur. The other had on a white coat and white duck trousers. They looked up inquiringly.

"Sheedley?" Tait inquired, looking at the one in the white coat.

The man nodded. "Yeah."

Tait came in the room and said: "I want to talk to you a minute about that ambulance call you had at Fourteenth and High last night."

Sheedley got up slowly. He was tall and bony, with protruding teeth and corn-colored hair that stuck up in startled tufts. He turned his full face towards Tait, and Tait saw that he had a beautiful black eye that made his whole head look lop-sided. The eye was the color of an over-ripe plum and swollen completely shut.

"You a friend of the guy we picked up?" Sheedley asked belligerently, putting his head down and taking a couple of shuffling steps forward like a boxer advancing out of his corner. "Are yuh, huh?"

"No," said Tait flatly. "But just supposing I was, what were you going to do about it?"

Sheedley stopped short and poked his head out like a startled turtle. He took another look at Tait's thick shoulders and dented nose.

"Well..." he said uncertainly.

Tait rolled his shoulders a little and took a step forward. Sheedley backed up, swallowing with his mouth open. He looked like he had just bitten into a hot potato and was wishing he hadn't.

"Sit down," said Tait levelly.

"Well, now...." Sheedley said in an uneasy way. He sat down very gently, as though he didn't expect the chair would hold him up.

Tait looked at the driver. "Blow."

The driver blinked, startled. "Who? Me?"

"Yeah," Tait said in the same flat voice.

The driver started to smile and then changed his mind. "Why, sure," he said quickly. "Sure, friend. Excuse me." He got up, sidled carefully around Tait, ducked out the door.

Tait sat down in the chair he had vacated and stared narrowly at Sheedley. "Don't get tough with me," he said. "It makes me very nervous, and when I get nervous I'm liable to do something about it all of a sudden. Now what's your big bellyache?"

Sheedley swallowed a couple of times and got started in a whiningly injured voice. "Well, it's like this. We got a call to go out to Fourteenth and High. When we get out there, there is a big crowd and this bird layin' out on the pavement colder than a toad from a conk on his knob. It's a hit-run they tell us, and there's a cop that's found some dame that witnessed it, and she's givin' a description of the guy that was drivin' the car—"

Tait interrupted. "Wait a minute. You've got that wrong, haven't you? You mean a guy was givin' a description of the dame that was drivin' the car."

Sheedley shook his head positively. "Nope. It was a dame that was the witness, because I seen her. And it was a guy drivin' the hit-run car because I heard her describin' him to the cop."

"Huh!" said Tait, puzzled. "You sure you got the right accident? Fourteenth and High last night at six o'clock."

Sheedley nodded again. "Yup. So we load the bird that's knocked out in the wagon and start back to the hospital. I am putting a bandage on this bird's knob, when all of a sudden he comes to and sits up and says: 'Who hit me?' Like I said, I heard the description the dame gives the cop, so I give it to this bird. And then what does he do?" Sheedley paused dramatically.

"I'll bite," said Tait. "What did he do?"

"He goes nuts, that's what. He starts jumpin' up and down on the stretcher and wavin' his arms around and yells: 'Dandruff two grabs,' at the top of his voice."

"What?" Tait demanded incredulously. "Dandruff two grabs?"

"Yup," said Sheedley firmly, "That's just what he said. I remember because that's why I think he's nuts. There ain't no sense to yellin' things like that. Although guys sometimes yell pretty funny things when they're comin' out from under. But that isn't the worst of what happened."

"Go ahead," Tait said numbly. "What else?"

"Well, like I say, I think the guy is nuts, and so I push him back on the stretcher and tell him to take it easy. And then what do you think he does?"

"I pass," said Tait. "What did he do?"

Sheedley pointed to his eye. "That's what. He hauls off and slams me in the eye and opens the back door of the ambulance and jumps out and runs like hell."

Tait blew out his breath in a loud snort. He put his hands on his knees and leaned forward and glared narrowly at Sheedley.

"You wouldn't try to fool me, would you, mister?"

Sheedley held up his right hand, palm out. "God's truth. That's just what he done. You can ask the driver—the one that was just in here. He can tell when the doors of the ambulance are open. And as soon as this bird opens 'em, the driver stops the car. But before he can get out and come around in back and dig me out from under a couple of stretchers and some bottles of medicine and a couple of instrument cases and find out what the hell is happening, the guy has disappeared."

Tait sat back in his chair and scratched his jaw, squinting

thoughtfully. "This is the screwiest one I ever ran into. You get this guy's name?"

Sheedley shook his head. "Nope. Didn't have no identification on him at all. He was a great big guy with curly blond hair. Real good lookin'."

"You remember the description the dame gave the cop—the description of the driver of the hit-run car?"

"Sure. The dame said it was a little short guy in a Ford coupé. She said he had a dished-in pan and a thick ear and a lot of gold teeth, and he wore a hat that had a red band with a little blue feather in it. She saw him plain, she said, because he stopped the car for a second and poked his dome out the window to look back at this bird he knocked over, and he was right under a street light. But she forgot to take his number." Sheedley had regained some of his courage by this time, and he asked curiously: "What do you want to know all this for?"

Tait pushed out his jaw and screwed his face up into a hard-boiled leer. "I got an idea the big bird that socked you is the same one that's been makin' passes at my wife. When I find him I'm gonna tear him up like a piece of paper."

Sheedley looked pleased. "Gee, I hope so,"

"You hope what?" Tait demanded bluntly.

Sheedley blinked and swallowed. "Don't get me wrong," he said hastily. "I didn't mean I hoped he'd been makin' passes at your wife. I meant I hoped you tore him up like a piece of paper. Only you better watch out, because he can hit like a ten-ton truck. Look what he did to my eye, and he swung on me when he was sittin' down."

COMING OUT OF the hospital, Tait got in his battered

old Cadillac touring car, which was parked beside a fire hydrant on the street that ran alongside the hospital. He sat in the driver's seat for quite a while, motionless, staring straight ahead through the moisture streaked windshield while cars slipped past with a whir and spatter of wet tires and the rain tapped gently on the taut canvas top.

"Huh!" he said to himself finally in a puzzled tone. "Dandruff two grabs... Dandruff two grabs...."

Suddenly he stiffened, and his eyes opened very wide. He snapped his fingers loudly and swore in a tight whisper. Jerking the paper he had bought earlier out of the pocket of his trench coat, he folded it back to the front page. Headlines ran blackly across two columns in the center.

JURY FREES TAGREBS, HARDEN, SARDI

Zanif Tagrebs, Charles Harden, and Miguel Sardi were acquitted yesterday of the charge of murdering Charles LaSalle, teller, in a hold-up of the Workman's Saving Bank at Junction Bend on August 17th. District Attorney Benjamin Daley said that in view of the jury's action he would not attempt to hold the defendants on the alternate charge of robbery....

Slowly Tait folded the paper up again. He pushed out his lower lip and tugged at it absently with a thumb and forefinger, squinting.

"Hmm," he said thoughtfully. "Dandruff two grabs. Zanif Tagrebs. Now I wonder...."

THERE WAS A fat man trying to lead the orchestra with an empty glass in one hand and a long bar spoon in the other.

The small dance-floor was crowded, and couples bumped into him constantly, but he didn't seem to mind at all. He swayed back and forth gently with a beautifully peaceful expression on his round, pink face.

Tait detoured around him, dodged a hurrying waiter, wiggled through a line of dancing couples, and got to the small table in back of the palm in the corner beside the orchestra's platform.

"Hello, MacDuff," he said.

MacDuff had his hat down over his eyes and was staring at the top of the table in front of him. He had both hands on the table. One held a beer mug, the other a pretzel. MacDuff didn't seem to know what he was going to do with either one. He looked up at Tait out of blankly dull eyes and said:

"Hello, Jake. Sit."

Tait held up one finger at a waiter, pulled a chair back. There was a big crowd in the place for an afternoon, and noise hammered back and forth between the walls deafeningly, and tobacco smoke swirled in endless blue streamers, and the light clinking of glassware was a muted undertone to the brassy wham of the orchestra.

Tait put his elbows on the table, leaned closer. "Too bad about that Junction Bend business, MacDuff."

MacDuff said: "Yeah," lifelessly. He had a long solemn face that was uncannily expressionless. He didn't move his lips when he talked.

"I didn't pay much attention at the time," Tait went on. "What's the low-down?"

MacDuff stared at the beer mug and the pretzel for quite a while as though he were figuring out how much of an effort it would be to talk. Finally he said heavily:

"Two of the boys, Harden and Sardi, are from Toledo. Came down this way on a vacation when things got warm up there. Neither one has a record, but they're known. While they were loafing around, they stumbled on to this bank at Junction Bend. It looked easy. Small bank—isolated—carries lots of dough to cash pay checks when the two factories at the Bend pay off. They took in this Zanif Tagrebs on the deal. He poses as an Egyptian. Used to be a wrestler until dames and liquor and weed parties softened him up. He drove the car." MacDuff stopped and sighed heavily.

"What happened?" Tait asked.

MacDuff sighed again. "We been thinkin' for quite a while that bank was a nice one to knock over, so we were watchin' it pretty close. One of the radio cars got there a minute and a half after they got out of the bank. Picked up their trail and were right after 'em. But they slipped the radio car in traffic and switched cars. They left their guns, masks, and the dough in the first car—a hot one. When we picked 'em up a half hour later, they were clean. We couldn't find anybody to identify 'em for sure. They were smart, those boys. Wore gloves all the time. Wasn't a print in that first car."

"How about the guy they knocked over?" Tait inquired.

"That was the worst part. He was only a kid—about twenty-four—and they didn't have to do it. He had his hands up and wasn't resisting. They just cracked down on him for no good reason. We're pretty sure it was Sardi did that."

Tait sipped his beer thoughtfully. "Keeping track of them?"

MacDuff shook his head. "The whole business gives me a bellyache. I don't want any more of it."

"Got any idea where I could find Tagrebs?"

MacDuff moved the beer mug a little. "Had a joint down on Rio when we picked him up. May still have it. *Regal Arms Apartments* in the 1700 blocks somewhere."

THE REGAL ARMS was a small apartment house, crowded close up against the corner, as though the architect had been determined to use up every available inch of the lot on which it stood. Wet dirt grated unpleasantly under Tait's feet as he went up the worn stone steps. He pushed a door open, went into a small, dark little lobby. The tile floor had once been white, and the dirt on it was more noticeable than that on the steps.

Along one wall there were rows of brass mail boxes with cards in the slots in front of them. Tait ran his fingers down the rows and found that Zanif Tagrebs had apartment number 112.

Tait went up four steps and was in a long hall that ran back darkly. The air here was heavy, thick, cold. A radio snored faintly in one of the apartments, and the floor boards creaked weirdly under Tait's feet as he walked back along the hall, watching the brass numerals on the regularly spaced doors.

He found 112 and stopped in front of it, listening. He could hear no sound from inside. He knocked softly on the door. There was still no sound, no movement from inside the apartment.

Tait straightened up, looked warily up and down the empty hall. Then he took a ring of skeleton keys from his pocket and began to work on the lock. It didn't take him long. The bolt clicked, and he pushed the door open slowly. He pushed it until it was clear back against the wall, and then he put his head carefully inside. He stiffened suddenly and blew out his breath in a little hissing noise.

He was looking cross-wise through a small entry hall, through another door into the living-room. He could see only part of the living-room floor, but there was a hand there on the floor, the arm extending back out of his line of vision.

The hand was clenched into a fist, had gathered up some of the rug in its grip. It didn't move, that hand. Didn't move at all. It was rigidly tense.

Tait moistened his lips with his tongue, standing very still in the doorway. Then he took a short barreled .38 revolver out of the waistband of his pants. The hammer clicked loudly under his thumb. But the rigid hand on the floor didn't relax its grip on the rug.

Tait reached behind him, not taking his eyes from the living-room door, and closed the outside door carefully, bolted it. Very softly he walked across the hall. He stood close to the wall and pushed the drape aside a little.

He moved the drape back and forth with his finger, but there was still no sound from inside the living-room. After a little, he put his head around the corner of the door.

Tagrebs was sprawled out in the middle of the floor, face down, like a baseball player sliding for the home plate. His neck was twisted at a grotesquely sharp angle, and his tongue protruded bluely between his gold front teeth. Something had smashed his nose, and it had bled a little bit down over his lips. He had been dead for quite a while.

Tait could look across the living-room into the bedroom. There was an open window in the far wall, and under the window a little pool of rain water had gathered on the floor, and the curtain was dripping wet.

Tait relaxed then and walked into the living-room. The place hadn't been disturbed any. He went on into the bedroom. The bed was made. The room was in order. It looked as though it had been in order for a long time. It had the musty air of vacancy.

Tait came back into the living-room and stared down at Tagrebs' body for a moment. His face was soberly thoughtful. Finally he let himself out of the apartment again, carefully wiping his fingerprints off the door with his handkerchief.

Tait walked up the block, went into the drug-store on the corner, entered one of the phone booths at the back. He put a nickel into the slot, dialed a number.

A masculine voice said: "Police Department."

"Give me the traffic squad," Tait requested.

There was a click, then another voice said: "Traffic bureau."

"I'd like to speak to Lieutenant Larsen," Tait said.

"Just a moment."

Tait waited patiently, and finally a thickly jovial voice said: "Larsen speaking."

"This is Jake Tait, Larsen."

"Hi-yuh, Jake. What you want now—a ticket fixed?"

Tait said: "Not this time. Do me a favor, Larsen. Find out the address of the woman who was a witness to the hit-run accident on Fourteenth and High last night about six."

Larsen chuckled. "If you're thinking of fixing that, Jake, there's no need. The victim ran out on us. That was the funniest one I ever heard. The victim hauled off and slammed the orderly—"

Tait interrupted impatiently: "Yeah, I know. But I still want the witness' address. Find it for me, will you?"

"Sure. Wait a minute."

There was a long wait. Tait took a pencil from his vest pocket and drew scrawling pictures on the wall of the booth, squinting in a preoccupied way. Then Larsen's voice said:

"Jake? It's 4332½ West Clover—a bungalow court, I think. The name is Kaylor."

Tait said: "Thanks. I'll be seeing you soon."

TAIT WENT ALONG a neatly trimmed privet hedge, sparklingly green from the moisture on the leaves, went in through a neatly trellised white arch. He was in a square court paved with red flag-stone. In the center of the court a stone frog spouted a thin, arching stream of water into a small stone pool. There were eight small bungalows, white and neat and square, all exactly alike, facing each other across the court. Each had a small cement porch on one side, a hedge across the front.

A thin bald-headed man in shirt sleeves was sweeping wet leaves off the porch of the front bungalow on the right in a very tired and discouraged way. When he heard Tait's footsteps, he stopped sweeping and leaned on the broom wearily.

"No peddlers allowed in here, mister," he said sadly.

Tait said: "Which one is 4332½—Kaylor?"

The tired man lifted his arm as though it were an immense effort and pointed to the next bungalow. "There."

As Tait turned around a man came out on the porch of the bungalow the tired man's drooping finger indicated. He was dressed in an expensive gray suit that had been cut to fit his immensely wide shoulders, his flat hips. He was carrying a small traveling case in his left hand, had his right hand in his trousers pocket. He was very good looking, with a wide jaw, handsomely even features. He was smiling in a pleasantly amiable way and whistling softly through his teeth.

He came down the steps of the bungalow, and the tired man said:

"Here's a guy wants to see you, Mr. Kaylor."

The big man said: "Yes?" pleasantly and swung around to face Tait. It was all done very easily and smoothly, and the big man was still smiling in his amiable way as he brought his right hand out of his pocket and swung a quick, slashing blow at Tait. Tait saw the fist coming, caught a wink of metal, knew that the big man wore a pair of brass knuckles.

Tait had no time to dodge, no time to bring his arm up to block. He did the best he could. He slackened his knees, tried to roll his head sidewise. The brass knuckles caught him on the cheek, and the force of the blow spun him half around, knocked him staggering.

The big man was after him like a cat. He was incredibly fast. Tait dug his heels in, got his guard half up, his head down. The second blow caught him high on the forehead. It was a terrific round-house swing, and it knocked Tait clear off his feet.

He turned over in mid-air, seeing the whole bungalow court spin slowly around like some queer kaleidoscopic picture. Seeing the tired man, still there on the porch, leaning on his broom with his mouth sagging vacantly open and his eyes bulging in unbelieving astonishment. Then he hit the ground, catching himself on his hands.

Without setting himself or hesitating for a second, the big man swung his foot, kicked him in the side of the head. Tait fell flat, and the big man jumped easily over him, dodged into the open space between two of the bungalows.

It had all happened amazingly fast. It had been no more than five seconds from the time the big man had said: "Yes?" until he was out of sight.

Tait got up. There was a tremendous roaring in his ears, and the ground kept tipping up dizzily under him. He staggered around in a little circle, stumbling, sawing clumsily at the air with his arms, trying to get his balance. He made for the space between the two bungalows on stiff legs that had no feeling in them at all. He stumbled along a narrow cement walk, crashed through a hedge, and was in a narrow little alley. There was no one in sight either way.

He was standing there, swaying a little, when the tired man poked his bald head cautiously into view, then squeezed through the hedge. He was holding Tait's hat in his hand. He brushed it off carefully, not saying anything, and then handed it to Tait.

Tait took it, started to say something, spat blood, and then said: "Thanks," thickly.

"Gosh," said the tired man in a small, awed voice. "Gosh, did he hit you!"

Tait spat some more blood, felt carefully inside his mouth with a forefinger.

The tired man shook his head slowly, watching him. "Gosh, I never see anybody get hit like that and get right up again. Brass knucks, too."

Tait grunted painfully, withdrew his finger from his mouth. He seemed to notice the tired man for the first time. He grinned, and a little blood seeped out of the corner of his mouth.

"I can take it," he said. He turned around and walked down the alley, still staggering a little.

The tired man stood there, staring after him open-mouthed. "Gosh," he said, scratching his bald head. "What a guy!"

TAIT CAME OUT of the back room of the drug-store and went into one of the phone booths. He had a white strip of court plaster across his forehead, another across his cheek from the lobe of his ear to the corner of his mouth. His cheek on that side was badly swollen. His whole face was dark, flushed with blood, and his eyes glittered flatly. He looked like he was holding himself in with an immense effort, and when he slid the nickel into the slot on the telephone, his hand shook a little. He dialed the number of the Police Department and asked to be connected with Lieutenant Larsen.

"This is Jake Tait again," he said when Larsen answered. "You remember that address you gave me?"

"Yes," said Larsen. "Sure, Jake. Why?"

"You sure it was the right one?"

"Why, yes," Larsen answered, puzzled. "I've got it right here. 4332½ West Clover, and the name was Kaylor. What's the matter?"

Tait said: "That isn't the address of the witness. That's the address of the guy that got hit."

"But—but" Larsen stuttered blankly. "That couldn't be! We didn't get his address!"

"You got it now," Tait said. "That's it. We just had a little skirmish, and he knocked out two of my teeth with a pair of brass knucks and scrammed. He's the guy that poked the orderly on the ambulance, all right. He answers to the description, and anyway there aren't two guys in this town that can hit like he can. Is MacDuff there?"

"Y-yes," Larsen said. "He came in about a half hour ago. He's tight. He was pretty disgusted with how that Junction Bend case came out. He spent a lot of time on it. He told me he was going out and get drunker than seven hundred dollars, and he did. He's asleep now."

"Sober him up," Tait ordered. "Tell him that I've got a lead on that Junction Bend business—a new angle. Tell him to stick around there, and I'll call him back as soon as I get something."

"What are you going to do?" Larsen asked.

Tait said: "I'm after that guy that socked me. I want another chance at him. He caught me when I wasn't expecting it this time. The next time she'll be different."

"But wait—"

Tait hung up the receiver. He opened the door of the booth and stepped outside. Reaching in his vest pocket, he brought out several cards. He shuffled them over until he found one of his own. On it was written in pencil the name, "Alice Glendon," and the address "Apartment 322 *Fenwood Arms*, Elm and Twenty-second."

HE TURNED DOWN off Twenty-first and parked the Cadillac at the curb about halfway down the block. He got out and walked down towards the corner. It was getting dark now, and the street lights were like fuzzy yellow balls with the mist rolling around them thickly. There was the warm smell of food cooking from some house close-by and the drip and spatter of rain water falling from the trees to the pavement.

Tait turned in a walk, went up a steep, narrow flight of stone steps that took a quarter turn and ended in front of a huge plateglass door bordered with fancy grille work. He went into a small, warm-looking lobby with tall parchment shaded lamps in each of the four corners and a small desk with a switchboard behind it against one wall. There was no one at the desk, nor in the big black leather chairs that sat against the other walls.

Tait went quietly across the thick greenish rug, quietly up the stairs. He went along a narrow hall for a little way, saw that the first door was numbered 201. He went back to the stairs, went up another flight. He walked along a hall exactly the same as the one below. His feet made no sound on the thick rug, and he could hear the faint stirs of movement from the apartments on both sides of the hall. He went around a corner, kept on down to the end of the hall. Three twenty-two was the last apartment.

Tait stood looking at the door for a moment, rocking back and forth slowly on the balls of his feet. He pushed out his lower lip, pulled at it absently, then winced as it jerked the cut on his cheek. He took his revolver out of his waistband, slid it into the pocket of his trench coat. Then he knocked softly on the door.

There was a cautious stir of movement from inside the apartment, and then a voice said softly:

"Yes? Who is it?"

Tait moved a little away from the door, but he didn't say anything. He leaned forward, shifting his weight, ready to jump.

The voice said again, louder: "Who is it?"

Tait didn't answer. He drew in his breath, held it.

There was a light click, and the door opened an inch. Tait jumped for it, lowering one shoulder. There was a jar, a frightened gasp, and the door slammed bade. Tait pushed inside the room, caught the door, closed it quickly behind him. He stood with his back to it, grinning.

"Hello, Alice," he said amiably.

Alice Glendon put the back of her hand up to her soft red mouth and took a step backward. Her blue eyes were widely staring, terrified, and she was breathing in short, broken gasps.

"Don't be scared," Tait said soothingly. "I just thought I'd drop in and report—"

He stopped talking. The big man was standing in the door that led to the bedroom. He had his coat off now, and his black suspenders, arching up over his white shirt, made his chest and shoulders look even bigger than before. Now that he had his hat off, Tait could see that he had a white bandage on the back of his head. He was holding an automatic in his right hand, and he was smiling a little in his pleasant way.

"Take your hands out of your pockets," he said in a quiet voice. "Very slowly."

Tait was standing turned half away from him. He couldn't do anything else. He brought his hands out of his pockets, raised them shoulder high.

The big man came a couple of short steps in the room, and another man came out of the bedroom, slid along the wall, watching Tait with unblinking black eyes. This second man was about medium height with swarthily dark skin, sleekly black hair that came down to a point on his forehead. He grinned constantly, as though the expression was fixed on his face and frozen there. The smoothly gliding manner in which he moved reminded Tait of a snake.

"How'd you get here?" the big man asked.

"Followed you," said Tait. His face was carefully wooden, although his eyes were very narrow, very shiny, very watchful.

"Why follow me?" the big man inquired. He still talked in the same casually pleasant voice, but the muzzle of the automatic was very steady.

Tait said: "I'm a detective."

"You lie," the big man said quietly. "I thought you were the first time I ran into you, but you wouldn't have come here alone if you were. And you didn't follow me here. Nobody did."

Tait shifted his feet a little. "You boys are cutting up pretty fancy for a couple of guys that just slid out from under a murder charge, aren't you?"

"You know who we are?" the big man asked.

Tait nodded. "Sure. You're Harden, and your snaky pal here is Sardi."

The big man nodded, smiling easily. "That's right. And do you know her, too?" He indicated Alice Glendon with a flick of his left hand.

Tait shook his head. "No."

"He's lying," said Sardi. He flicked his tongue quickly over his thin lips, stared at Tait with viciously unblinking eyes. "He knows her. He spoke to her when he came in. She tipped him to this spot. She tipped him to your other spot." He looked at Alice Glendon. "Didn't you. Honey?"

She was standing with her back pressed hard against the wall, rigidly tense. The color had gone out of her face and left it paper-white. She braced her legs, pushing herself harder against the wall. She swallowed twice before she could say anything.

"No," she said, shaking her head quickly. "No, no."

"Oh, yes you did, Honey," Sardi contradicted in his hissingly soft voice. "You tried to double-cross us. Do you think that's right, Honey?" He slid along the wall towards her. His eyes glittered like narrow pieces of black jet.

Alice Glendon brought her right hand out from behind her back. She held a short, flat .25 automatic. She pushed the automatic straight out in front of her at arm's length, pointed it at Sardi.

"I'm going to shoot," she said as though it were a great effort to get the words out. There was a little streak of blood, very red against her pale cheek, at the corner of her mouth where she had bitten her lips.

"You—" Sardi snarled, and jumped for her.

The little automatic smacked sharply, like a loud hand-clap. Sardi screamed and straightened up and then arched his back as though he were going to bend double backwards. He put both hands up to his face and blood spilled out between his clutching fingers.

Harden moved sidewise, swinging the automatic away from Tait towards Alice Glendon. Tait took one short step and dived for his legs, turning himself in the air like a football player taking out an opponent. He hit Harden just above the knees, and the big man fell headfirst over him, hit the floor in a sliding sprawl.

Tait rolled free, got up to his knees, dug for the .38 in the pocket of his trench coat. Sardi, walking blindly backwards with his hands still clutched tight over his face, tripped over him, fell down heavily on top of him.

Tait was pinned down on the floor with his right hand cramped under him. He looked up and saw Harden, not ten feet away, sitting up and facing him. Harden was smiling a little, still, and he was aiming his automatic carefully at Tait's head.

Tait saw the big forefinger whiten at the knuckle and knew that he couldn't shift Sardi's lax weight in time to get his own .38 out. He closed his eyes and tensed himself, and there was a sharp flat report.

Tait opened his eyes and saw Harden slowly trying to turn his big body around. There was another sharp report, and Harden opened his eyes very widely and stared at Tait in a blankly surprised way. Then he closed his eyes and lay back on the floor, very gently and easily, as though he had decided to go to sleep.

The door into the hall was open about six inches. There was a hand poked through into the room. It was Alice Glendon's hand, and her fingers were still clutched tightly around the .25 automatic. There was a wispy spiral of powder smoke curling lazily up from the blunt little muzzle of the automatic.

As Tait watched, the hand withdrew out of sight, and the door closed very softly, and Alice Glendon's high heels tap-tapped hurriedly as she ran down the hall.

TAIT ROLLED OUT from under Sardi. Sardi was laxly limp. His arms flopped lifelessly, and he stared up at the ceiling with eyes that were glassily wide in the bloody mask of his face. Harden's head was pillowed on his arm. His eyes were shut, and his mouth was open a little bit. He looked like he was sleeping peacefully, except for the fact that his chest didn't move.

Tait got up stiffly and stood staring down at the two of them. He realized suddenly that he was clammy with perspiration and that his tongue felt thick and swollen and dry in his mouth.

Suddenly someone in the next apartment started to pound on the wall. There was a yell from out in the hall, and a woman on the floor above opened her window and screamed frantically.

The noise brought Tait to himself with a jerk. He walked across the room, stepping carefully over Harden's body, and picked up the telephone from its cradle on the stand near the door.

"Police," he said into the mouthpiece and then, after a short pause: "Lieutenant MacDuff. Homicide. Make it snappy."

There was another wait, and Tait could hear the loud voices in the hall. The voices were coming slowly down the hall towards the apartment.

MacDuff's voice said irritably: "What?"

"This is Jake Tait."

"You!" MacDuff snarled. "You're the guy that told Larsen to sober me up! What's the idea—"

"Shut up," Tait said shortly. "I'll do the talking. You listen. I'm in Harden's apartment. Harden and Sardi are here. They're dead. Tagrebs is in his apartment down on Rio. He's dead."

It took MacDuff quite a while to get that. He was silent for as long as it would take a man to count to five slowly, then he said:

"Dead?"

Tait said: "All three."

"Dead," MacDuff repeated, as though he couldn't quite get adjusted to the idea.

There were whispers outside the apartment door. Someone rattled the latch cautiously.

Tait said: "Here's what happened as near as I can figure it. Tagrebs was sore as hell at Sardi and Harden because they pulled him in on this bank job and got him saddled with a murder rap and damn' near got him hung, and he didn't get a cent out of it. So he laid for Harden and tried to run him down with his car. That was the hit-run accident at Fourteenth and High. Harden found out it was Tagrebs that knocked him over, and he went high-tailing after him hell-bent because he was afraid Tagrebs would keep after him until he got him, and it was a question of safety to get him first. He laid for Tagrebs in his apartment, smacked him with a pair of brass knucks, laid him out, and then cracked his neck for him. I walked into the picture over here just as Harden and Sardi were getting ready to scram, and we had a little set-to, and first thing you know, they were both dead."

Somebody started pounding on the door. The voices in the hall swelled out louder.

"Yeah," said MacDuff. "Yeah, that's fine. That explains everything except how you got on to that hit-run case in the first place, and how it happens that the address the witness gave was the address of Harden's hide-out on West Clover, and how you found the place where you are now, and a few other little things like that."

Tait said: "I'm guessing now, but it's the only possible answer. Sardi had a gal. She cased their jobs for them. She ran on to LaSalle, the guy who got shot in the bank job, somewhere and got acquainted with him. That's why Sardi and Harden picked that bank. But LaSalle was a pretty nice boy, young and pretty dumb maybe, and he took the gal seriously. And she began to take him seriously, too. Sardi got wind of what was going on, and that's why he knocked over LaSalle when they robbed the bank.

"The gal's not so dumb. She knew what happened. So she

worked on Tagrebs, got him sore at the other two. I think she was probably with Tagrebs when he tried to run Harden down. When it didn't work, she claimed she was a witness and gave Tagrebs' description to the cops, knowing that Harden would hear about it and guess that it was Tagrebs that had tried to knock him over. She knew Harden would get Sardi and start after Tagrebs with all four feet. She gave the address of one of Harden's hang-outs. Then she came around to me and put me on the case, giving me the address of Harden's other hide-out. She knew Tagrebs would have a run-in with Harden and Sardi, and that somebody would get themselves killed. She didn't care who, since she figured they had all done her dirty by knocking off LaSalle. She hoped I'd be close enough on the trail, what with the lead she gave me, to pin the killing on whoever was left.

"But Harden worked faster than she expected, and just by dumb luck she and Sardi were over here at his place getting ready to scram when I turned up. That tipped the lid off, and the fireworks started."

"Um," said MacDuff thoughtfully. "The gal there now?"

"Nope," said Tait.

"Ah," said MacDuff, relieved. "You don't have any idea where she went, do you?"

"Nope."

"Um," said MacDuff. "You can't remember her name, can you? Or what she looked like?"

Tait grinned a little. "Nope."

"Well," said MacDuff in a pleased voice. "I guess we can't find her then, can we?"

Tait chuckled. "I guess not. You're not fooling me, sonny boy.

You were tipped that somebody was going to crack that bank. That's why the radio car got clear out there so fast. And you know and I know, now, who tipped you. Only you muffed the job, so she started out on her own and did it up brown."

Something heavy battered on the door, and a harsh voice said: "Open up! This is the law!"

Tait said quickly into the telephone: "Hold the wire. Some of your pals are outside, and if you don't talk to them, they're liable to start pushing me around."

About the Author

WE HAVE MR. Davis' own word for
it that he is large. Since it is virtu-
ally impossible to pry him loose
from his beloved California, we
have never had the pleasure of
meeting this exceedingly success-
ful author of ours. So we wrote
him, demanding to know who he
was. Shortly we received a self-study,
captioned *Norbert Davis: His Life and
Works.* We quote:

"When you read one of these writer-biography sketches,
you get the idea that the bird who is writing about himself is
a pretty smart guy. Don't believe it. I know a hundred writers,
and they are mostly dopes. But not me. Oh, no! I'm so full of
brains I'm constantly out-smarting myself.

"Aside from that, I'm six feet five inches tall, weigh two
hundred and fifteen pounds, have a face like a gargoyle and
the disposition of a tired tarantula. I don't have any dislikes. I
love everybody and everything, but most of all I love sports—
spectator sports. I go for any game where I can sit down and
watch the other guy work, and shout: 'Thatta boy,' or 'Well
played, old chap,' from time to time.

"I served two terms in college—four years at the University
of California and three years at Stanford, where my characters
picked up their legal lore.

"My motto is: All editors are crazy, but I love them dearly—each and every one.

"So long, folks. See you again soon."

In his modesty Mr. Davis has been all too brief, and the sketch requires some amplification. We've heard, for instance, that he first started to write when he was studying law at Stanford. Fiction was to be a sideline, for the serious side of the man was dedicated to the law. But the story habit got a firm and permanent grip on him, and so here he is today, busily turning out his fast and cleverly plotted novels. And plenty of us are glad that Mr. Davis could not shake off the urge to write.

The Works, which Mr. Davis says nothing whatever about, are numerous. At least two of them—"Gunsmoke Case for Mayor Cain" and "Sand in the Snow"—have been bought by the movies. The pictures haven't yet been produced. Then there have been serials a-plenty, in *Argosy* and elsewhere; and Mr. Davis has several books to his credit. For a man who claims that he constantly out-smarts himself, he's done pretty well; there apparently is much to be said for a tired tarantula.

So long, Norbert Davis. Writers aren't sane, either.